Something in Jake's mind clicked. Oliver had told him to be on the lookout for anything new, and Invince, well. . . that was new. Was it just a coincidence that Gaia had started acting insecure and timid at around the same time that half of New York City was dosed with fake adrenaline? It seemed like a long shot—but then again, he didn't have any shorter shots left.

D1211420

Don't miss any books in this thrilling series:

FEARLESS™

Available from SIMON PULSE

For orders other than by individual consumers, Simon & Schuster grants a discount on the purchase of **10 or more** copies of single titles for special markets or premium use. For further details, please write to the Vice-President of Special Markets, Pocket Books, 1260 Avenue of the Americas, New York, NY 10020-1586, 8th Floor.

For information on how individual consumers can place orders, please write to Mail Order Department, Simon & Schuster Inc., 100 Front Street, Riverside, NJ 08075.

FEARLESS™

EXPOSED

FRANCINE PASCAL

SIMON PULSE
New York   London   Toronto   Sydney

If you purchased this book without a cover, you should be aware that this
book is stolen property. It was reported as "unsold and destroyed" to the
publisher and neither the author nor the publisher has received any payment
for this "stripped book."

This book is a work of fiction. Any references to historical events, real
people, or real locales are used fictitiously. Other names, characters, places,
and incidents are the product of the author's imagination, and any resemblance
to actual events or locales or persons, living or dead, is entirely coincidental.

First Simon Pulse edition September 2004

Copyright © 2004 by Francine Pascal

Cover copyright © 2004 by 17th Street Productions,
an Alloy company.

SIMON PULSE
An imprint of Simon & Schuster Children's Publishing Division
1230 Avenue of the Americas, New York, NY 10020

Produced by 17th Street Productions,
an Alloy company
151 West 26th Street
New York, NY 10001

All rights reserved, including the right of reproduction
in whole or in part in any form.
For information address 17th Street Productions,
151 West 26th Street, New York, NY 10001.

Fearless™ is a trademark of Francine Pascal.

Printed in the United States of America
10 9 8 7 6 5 4 3 2 1

Library of Congress Control Number: 2004100273
ISBN: 0-689-86918-5

To Sabrine Mrabet

For a long time—in fact, for as long as I can remember—I thought I was a freak.

Forget "thought." I *was* a freak. I *am* a freak.

Doctors weren't sure what was wrong with me or what had transpired in my genetic code, but somehow, I was literally incapable of feeling fear. I didn't have the gene for it. Some sort of genetic mutation.

See? A freak. Sideshow attraction. Ship me off to the carnival.

I hated it. I hated myself and all of the icky by-products of being different. I hated the fact that my father had trained me to kick ass. Sure, pounding the crap out of some low-level street thug is satisfying, but I always dreamed of being a girlie-girl. Being able to thwart a mugger didn't take away the sting of being shunned by my classmates, who thought—rightly so—that I was oddly aggressive and always involved in one shady incident after another. From the days of elementary school, when my teacher scheduled a conference with my father to discuss my "combative tendencies," I was always the outsider.

And the social implications were only the tip of the dysfunctional iceberg. As a result of these attributes, people were—*are*—always after me. Always hurting the people who are important to me. Someone's always out to get me, manipulate me, dissect me. Like my genetic makeup is some sort of prize to be attained and exploited. No wonder my father, agent extraordinaire, worried so much when I was a kid. He knew what was in store for me.

So yeah—lack of fear? Not such a thrilling talent to have.

Lately, though, I've come to understand the benefits of my freakdom. Because lately, I've come to know fear.

Thanks to Dr. Rodke and his incredible medical advances, Gaia the Unfearing was temporarily transformed into a living, breathing regular girl. For the first time ever, I was really, truly afraid. Make that *terrified*. Everything I encountered—from the social mafia at the Village School to the prepubescent drug dealers in Washington Square Park, from the crazy homeless man outside Grey Dog Coffee to a random dog tied to a parking meter—*everything* scared me. I was petrified of my own shadow.

And let me tell you: it sucked.

'Cause the part of me that had grown used to ignoring the cheesy morons at school or that wouldn't be bullied by creeps in the park had also grown accustomed to taking all of those unsavories on, to the point where I almost thought of it as some sort of sick duty. If I saw a girl getting hassled in the park, I broke it up. Because I could. Because I wasn't afraid.

But with my newly manipulated

fear, I was helpless. Simpering. Practically useless. I ran from a fight while my boyfriend stood his ground. God only knows what that did to his opinion of me (yet another superfun source of anxiety in itself). I let my best friend (well, once best friend, anyway) and his new girlfriend get jumped. I didn't step in. Because I was *afraid*.

I let the FOHs, the ridiculous divas who—in their minds, anyway—run the Village School social scene—make me feel insecure. I sought out their approval. God help me, I wore a baby tee. The Village School saw my navel, no joke.

But worse than any of this was the fact that I let down my guard.

The foremost piece of information that my father passed along to me was to *never* let down my guard. He knew better than anyone that someone is almost always after us. He knew that I need to be constantly alert, to trust no one. And for as long as I've understood that, I've adhered to it. At least half the people who've made their ways into my life—Uncle Oliver, Ella, George, Natasha—have been out to get me.

So needless to say, suspicion has been a pretty useful emotion. One that's generally validated.

I'm not saying that fear reduced the element of suspicion. That's not the case at all. If anything, fear made me even more nervous around people, warier. Eventually I was checking my cell phone every three seconds to see if my boyfriend had called or, as previously mentioned, I was donning a baby tee rather than throwing it at Megan and her cronies and telling them where to shove it. But fear clouded my judgment. I started to doubt my own instincts, which, unfortunately, haven't failed me yet. I started to second-guess myself— the only person, ironically, that I can even trust. In fact, my own rational thought was clouded to the point that I actively sought out someone else's approval, someone else's direction, someone else's. . . *control*.

I'm not totally sure at what point I realized that my dependence on Skyler wasn't completely normal. It was like I looked up, and in the blink of an eye, it occurred to me that there was no good reason for turning over practically my whole persona to him. I've never relied on anyone before—namely because there was never anyone truly reliable in my life. Yet I was willing to give over all of my decisions to someone I barely knew. And why? Because he happened to come along and offer comfort on a night when I particularly needed it? Because he was authoritative? Because he was good-looking?

I'm sorry, not good enough.

That's exactly how it happened, though. The Rodkes came to town, and I met Liz and Chris, who were both amazing and

cool in an I'm-so-cool-I-don't-
even-notice-or-care-how-cool-I-
am kind of way. The antithesis
of the usual "worship me, I wear
Juicy Couture" attitude I
encounter at the hell dimension
otherwise known as high school.
And, stranger than fiction, the
two of them seemed to like me,
seemed to like hanging out with
me. Before I knew anything about
their father and his scientific
interests, I was well into the
Rodkes. I didn't even know who
Skyler was.

But yeah, from the minute I
laid eyes on him, there was something. Some spark between us—not
exactly sexual, but not exactly
brother-sister, either. Some completely unidentifiable, indefin-
able quality. And when I was
feeling nervous or jumpy (which,
let's face it, has lately been,
uh, *all the time*), he was reas-
suring. Calming. Authoritative.

Insistent.

And I went along with it.

When Skyler told me to blow

off Suko and stay all night in his apartment, I did it. When Skyler told me to shut off my cell phone and concentrate on our time together, I did it. When Skyler intimated that I'd be better off going to the prom with him and not with my—at least I think he still is—boyfriend, I agreed.

Huh?

Lately I've been feeling different. Like a veil has been lifted, a cloud of smoke has cleared, and I'm back in my own body. I don't know what's going on with Skyler—I can't for the life of me put my finger on what interest he has in using me as his own personal puppet. I don't think he wants to be my boyfriend. I don't think he's an undercover spy. I don't think he has the vaguest knowledge of the disparate plot twists that conspire to make my life so difficult. For the life of me, I can't get a handle on his line. But that's okay. I've got my wits about me again, and eventually I'm going to get to the bottom of

this. Because you know what?
Somehow I'm not afraid anymore.
Whatever Dr. Rodke did to me, I
don't think it was permanent.
Slowly but surely, I'm regressing
back to my usual freakishness. And
for the first time, being a freak
feels pretty damn good.

No, wait. That's not right.

It feels freakin' *great*.

She really
needed,
somehow, to
inexplicable
make **interest**
herself
care.

"SO, BELIEVE IT OR NOT, THE

Alpha Male

headmaster actually thought—Gaia? Are you even listening?"

"Huh?" At the sound of her voice Gaia snapped to attention. She realized she hadn't at *all* been listening to Skyler's story, an anecdote of boarding school boys gone wild or some such. Hardy har har. Big yuks. Wet toilet paper everywhere. Try though she might, she couldn't bring herself to care. She needed to, though. She really needed, somehow, to make herself care.

The problem was that now that Dr. Rodke's genetic manipulation seemed to be unraveling, Gaia wasn't finding herself especially dependent on Skyler. More than that, she was wholly suspicious of his interest in her. Now that she was thinking clearly again, she could see how strange it was that he had suddenly decided to take an interest in her, to watch over her, to protect her. He barely knew her, for chrissake. Please—people who *did* know her weren't that interested in her.

Gaia was going to have to get to the bottom of Skyler's inexplicable interest without arousing his suspicions, which meant, at least nominally, maintaining the helpless girlie-girl facade for at least a little longer. And that included feigning interest in his ridiculous stories.

But for how long?

As she envisioned the aging, graying version of herself, sixty years in the future, still patiently listening to Skyler's droning, the germ of an idea began to form in Gaia's mind.

Maybe there was a way to test Skyler, to push him, to see how much he could take before breaking. If she did everything in her power to challenge his patience, and if his tolerance remained boundless, she could know for sure that his motives weren't pure.

"Gaia? Do you not want to be here with me today? All afternoon you've seemed kind of distracted. I really wanted us to just have a fun day together, but if you're not interested, you know, just tell me." Gaia could hear the edge creep into Skyler's voice. If she was trying to push him, she was succeeding.

Good, she thought. *But watch it. It's a fine line.*

"I'm sorry, Skyler," she said, adopting a hasty, self-deprecating tone. "You've planned an amazing day for us. I don't know why I'm so spacey. Please don't take it personally."

In fact, Skyler had planned a wonderful afternoon. He had picked Gaia up from school that afternoon, taking in stride the fact that she had worn her hair up, even though he'd specifically asked her not to. (That actually hadn't been on purpose—Gaia had simply forgotten.) He had taken her to Gourmet Garage on Seventh Avenue, near her school, where they'd picked

12

up an array of luscious picnic treats: ripe, meaty olives packed in top-quality olive oil, heady cheeses, thick, crusty breads, and imported chocolates. He had bought a bottle of wine and taken her uptown to Central Park, where they now sat. She generally tended to spend the bulk of her time in Washington Square, so the change in scenery was welcome. It was a perfect, balmy day, and if Gaia hadn't been distracted by deeper concerns, she would have relished it.

But then again, maybe that was a good thing. Skyler certainly wasn't impressed by her inability to focus on him. If she irritated him enough, maybe she could draw him out. "I'm back, I promise," she asserted. "I want to hear the end of the story."

"It's okay," Skyler said reassuringly. "I can imagine it isn't such an interesting story to someone who wasn't there. Or, you know, someone who has emotionally matured beyond the age of twelve."

"I'm at least thirteen emotionally, so I guess I just missed the cutoff for your target audience." Gaia laughed. "But I do love a good wet-toilet-paper story."

"Well, okay," Skyler resumed. "See, the thing was that I *thought* the door was locked, but Trent— remember he was my roommate, and he was the one who had the rope and the Silly String—Trent had gotten the combination wr—"

"A movie!" Gaia exclaimed suddenly, deliberately

interjecting just as Skyler was warming to his story. "*That's* what we should do later on! I think there's a revival of *Streetcar Named Desire* playing at Film Forum. That'd be awesome." She glanced sideways at Skyler. Not only had she rather rudely cut him off, but she didn't know *any* `manly man` his age who would agree to seeing *that* movie.

For a moment she thought she saw Skyler's nostrils flare. She *thought* she saw a glimpse of fury flash across his chiseled face. But just as quickly as it was there, it vanished without a trace and was replaced by an affable grin.

"Is that really what you want to do today, Gaia?" Skyler said, seeming amused at the prospect. "It *is* such a beautiful day, after all. Not that it's a problem or anything. If that's what you want to do, that's what we'll do. Did you happen to notice what times the movie was playing?"

Gaia shook her head emphatically. "Nope. Just read about it in the *Voice* last week. But I was excited about it. It's always been one of my favorite movies."

This was `categorically untrue`. While she didn't have anything against the movie per se, it certainly wasn't one of her favorites. She'd seen it once when she was nine.

Skyler glanced at his watch. "Okay, well, maybe we should head on down there and get tickets. It's five now. There's probably a show at seven or eight.

We can kill time at—I don't know, are you hungry?"

Gaia shook her head again and indicated the array of food wrappers and containers littering the space before them on the ground. "Are you kidding?" she asked archly.

"Right, okay. Well, there's a coffee shop on Varick, you know. I think a Starbucks. But I don't mind a big corporate conglomerate." He winked. After all, Rodke and Simon Pharmaceuticals *was* a big corporate conglomerate. Skyler and his family were the embodiment of The Man. "Or I could take you to Vino, a little wine bar I know of."

"You sure you don't mind heading *all* the way back downtown again?" Gaia asked, infusing her voice with the plaintive lilt that, alas, she thought Skyler had probably grown accustomed to by now.

Skyler shrugged easily. "Of course not, Gaia. This day is all about you. About *us*," he corrected, wrapping an arm around her shoulders and hugging her close to him. He gathered up their trash, balled it together into the bottom of a Gourmet Garage bag, and tossed it, hoisting his slim Manhattan Portage messenger bag over his shoulder in one swift motion. "Let's go."

Thanks to the benefits of the A express, it wasn't twenty minutes later that Gaia and Skyler found themselves standing outside the Film Forum, surveying the crowd. And not a moment too soon, either. As it turned out, the movie was at six-thirty, and since it was such a popular pick, it was likely to sell out well before then. Gaia mused on the varied cross section of the New York City populace that had turned out on such an outdoorsy day. Punk rockers who looked like they hadn't showered in days stood behind quirky intellectual types whose tortoiseshell glasses sat perched at the tips of their noses. It was funny—Gaia wasn't sure where she stood on the spectrum, but if she fit in somewhere in the world, it was New York City—despite the fact that, or perhaps *because*, she actually *didn't* fit in.

Skyler seemed equally comfortable, equally happy to be having a very Manhattan afternoon, waiting on line outside an artsy movie house with a bunch of true New Yorkers. He didn't seem bothered in the least by Gaia's having broken up their impromptu picnic and dragged them back downtown.

Curious.

"Uh-oh," she hedged, biting her lip and assuming what she hoped was a woeful demeanor.

Skyler's gaze narrowed. "What?" he asked with more than a hint of annoyance.

"It's just, I forgot my membership card. We could get in for half price." She widened her eyes at Skyler innocently. "Do you think it'll sell out if I just run home—?"

"Of *course* it'll sell out if you 'just run home'!" Skyler mimicked impatiently, frustration seeping through his pores. He put his hands on his hips and softened visibly. "Gaia, it's very thoughtful of you to want to get us a discount, but I assure you, I can afford the ticket price. Next time we can use your card." He took her hand. "This way I get to play the alpha male."

Gaia shuddered inwardly, but she forced herself to smile back. The alpha male was exactly the problem. "Are you sure? I mean, it's no trouble. I can go back quickly—"

"Even for a superhero like you, Gaia, I think the line is moving a little too fast," Skyler said, effectively cutting her off. He had managed to sound playful again. A frizzy-haired woman standing in front of them in line shot Gaia a dirty look, suggesting that Gaia was being every bit as annoying as she imagined.

She was proud of her performance. But judging from Skyler's ability to keep his cool, it was clear that she had her work cut out for her. "You've been so understanding today, Skyler," Gaia practically cooed as they closed the gap between themselves and the ticket window. "You're so understanding every day." She wasn't entirely sure how to bat her eyelashes or she would have.

"No problem, Gaia," Skyler said sincerely. "That's what I'm here for." He slapped his wallet down onto the ticket seller's counter. "Two for the six-thirty show," he said.

"Oh!" Gaia shouted suddenly, as if she'd just had an incredibly random thought.

Skyler glanced at her warily. "What now?" he asked. His voice was light, but he did seem increasingly impatient.

"I, uh, really wanted some candy."

Skyler's gaze turned from hesitant to incredulous. "Well, good thing you're in the *movie theater*," he said slowly, "because I think they're equipped to handle your concession needs."

Gaia tilted her head to one side and stuck out her lower lip. "Come on. This is Film Forum. It's not like the local multiplex. They're not going to have any of the really good junky stuff. I think they only have muffins and croissants. Ten-dollar croissants," she added.

"Well, if you want a ten-dollar croissant, Gaia, that's fine. I mean, I have the cash. Not a big deal." Gaia had been sure this last little display would trigger at least a tiny crack in Skyler's composure. But no such luck.

"You're getting robbed blind here today," Gaia protested. "And I really have a sugar jones. I meant to stop off at a deli on the way here and pick up provisions, but I guess it slipped my mind."

"Weren't you *just* saying that you weren't hungry

because you ate so much in the park?" Skyler pointed out in a sudden fit of rationalism.

"Well, yeah, but it, uh, came on kinda quickly. Look," Gaia wheedled, "I'll just run across the street. You won't even miss me." She started toward the front door of the theater, aware that their little "lovers' spat" was drawing some local interest. As she passed by Skyler, she stomped on his foot "accidentally" for good measure. "Oops, sorry." She giggled.

"Gaia!" Skyler called after her, but the door was already swinging shut behind her.

"I'll get you some Maltesers," Gaia called over her shoulder. She had no idea how he even felt about Maltesers, and she was pretty sure he couldn't have cared less about them at the present time.

THREE HOURS, ONE TUB OF ARTIFICIAL-

Normal Circumstances

butter-flavored popcorn, one large Coke, and a bag of M&M's later, Gaia and Skyler strolled down Houston Street arm in arm, each slurping the dregs of an overpriced Starbucks espresso drink. Gaia gave a large gulp as she tossed her empty venti cup into the closest street trash can. "I do love a sugar rush," she asserted, qualifying the statement with a shy giggle.

"That much is obvious," Skyler said affectionately, finishing up his drink and tossing it as well. "I wouldn't have it any other way."

Gaia beamed. Skyler had been the perfect date all afternoon—too perfect. He had been smooth as satin no matter how many times she had tuned out while he was talking or interrupted him. He had agreed to whatever whim had struck her fancy. He hadn't complained when she crawled over him *again* during the movie under the premise of taking her fourth and final bathroom break.

No doubt about it, something was definitely up with Skyler.

Despite the fact that most of his plans involved having her at his side at all times, Gaia was more certain than ever that his goals weren't romantic. If Skyler'd had designs on her, he had also passed up some totally primo opportunities to put the moves on her. It had to be something worse than that, something more nefarious. And now that Gaia was certain something was up, she was finding herself eager—even excited—to get to the bottom of it.

Skyler, man, you underestimate me, she thought. *You have no idea who you're dealing with.*

Since her mom had been killed five years ago, Gaia had been attacked, chased, and confronted by some of the world's most dangerous criminal masterminds—several of whom she even considered family. And here she was, still, for better or for worse. She'd be damned if she'd let some rich prep school snob be her undoing.

She sidled up closer to him and sighed comfortably. *You're not even going to know what hit you,* she decided.

Gaia stumbled suddenly, hardly knowing what had hit *her.* Gazing up at Skyler, she'd stomped directly into a pedestrian walking toward them. She looked up, and her spirits instantly sagged. Standing in front of her, looking pressed and polished as always, was Megan. Megan had been one of the top-tier Friends of Heather back when Heather Gannis had ruled the Village School. But Heather had gone blind (*Just more fallout from my pathetically complicated life,* Gaia thought miserably), and Megan had ascended to the presidency of the social hierarchy.

Megan and her hen party couldn't seem to decide how they felt about Gaia. For the most part, they weren't impressed, but they were clearly somewhat taken by Gaia's admittedly inexplicable ability to land some very sought-after boyfriends. *Never mind that my relationships have a life span shorter than that of an ice-cream cone in August,* she thought glumly. And when Gaia and Liz had begun to hang out, the FOHs had taken a more acute interest in Gaia. But their interest tended to wax and wane depending on the circumstances of their own lives at any given moment, and at the present it seemed like they were dead set on seeing her falter. Which, hey— Gaia didn't think they'd have to wait long. That didn't mean she needed to put up with Megan and her bull, though.

Except that she did. For Skyler's sake. Skyler needed to think that Gaia was still caught fast in Megan's thrall, desperately seeking approval. *Ick,* Gaia thought, pasting an insecure grin on her face.

"Hi, Meegs," she said brightly. "Shopping?"

Megan shot Gaia a look that suggested she'd just taken a whiff of raw sewage. "No," she said dryly, "the bags are merely an illusion created by your mind's eye. Out with boyfriend number two, are we?" she asked snidely, indicating Skyler with a jerk of her head.

That was the other fun thing about the FOHs these days. They had the idea that Gaia was cheating on Jake.

Of course, Gaia was spending practically every waking moment with Skyler, while she hadn't seen all that much of Jake. And she had been keeping her cell phone shut off at Skyler's suggestion.

And then there was the matter of a little thing

called the prom. Which she had told Jake she would be attending with Skyler.

Come to think of it, it was easy enough to see how these rumors had gotten started.

Under normal circumstances, Gaia would have told Megan off and walked away or simply ignored her. But these weren't normal circumstances. Until she got to the bottom of the Skyler mystery, Gaia had to maintain her fearful persona on all fronts. Just to be on the safe side. "Skyler's just a friend, Megan, you know that," she said softly. "You know I'm totally into Jake."

Megan's eyes flashed with envious anger. "Actions speak louder than words, Gaia," she snapped. "You better hope that *Jake* knows how 'into' him you are. For the sake of your relationship," she warned darkly. "Not that I care," she added as an afterthought, flouncing off haughtily.

Like hell you don't, Gaia thought, knowing full well that once she was out of Gaia's range of vision, Megan would call half the school to report that she had caught Gaia Moore in the red-hot act of cheating on her man. She suppressed a sigh. She really *did* hope that Jake trusted her.

She hoped that Skyler did, too. She turned to him, smiling hesitantly. "Ugh." She grimaced. "She's awful."

"Thank God I've got you," he said.

"I'VE GOT AN IDEA," SKYLER

suggested, toying with the wineglass that sat in front of him on the wooden table.

Compliance

As promised, he had lured Gaia to Vino. It was the perfect place—tucked away in the cozy recesses of Bedford Street and too European to care about carding. The restaurant had a warm, relaxed vibe to it, and most nights patrons who were lucky enough to snag a table made a practice of camping out for hours at a time. Skyler had suggested a drink after their encounter with Megan, and Gaia had gladly accepted. Now she ran her fingers around the rim of her glass of Chianti. Getting drunk wasn't going to help her cause any. "What?" she asked, smiling at Skyler.

It wasn't too hard to smile at him. Despite her many misgivings, Gaia still found herself irresistibly drawn to Skyler's magnetic smile. He was a good-looking guy with a very easygoing charm. As far as undercover work went, this was pretty painless.

"Let's go back to my place and have a Brando fest. In the spirit of *Streetcar*, you know?" He grinned. "*Stella!*"

"I don't know," Gaia said reluctantly. "I'm really not supposed to stay out, and I've been pushing my luck with Suko lately. Eventually she's going to catch on to my 'studying with a friend' alibi."

"Come on, Gaia," Skyler insisted. "Since when does Gaia Moore care what anyone thinks of her? Do you really expect me to think you give a crap what Suko wants?"

Gaia shrugged. "Say what you want, but I do have to live with her. Her opinion does matter. She could make my life very difficult."

It was true: Suko could be a real battle-ax. But Gaia didn't care. She'd already figured out how to shimmy in and out of her bedroom window after curfew. And Zan, one of the other girls in the house, was always having unauthorized guests over. It wasn't as though it was impossible to circumvent the rules. Gaia simply didn't want to come across as *too* pliable.

Skyler took her hand. "Suko could make your life difficult," he agreed. "True. But I really want to be with you. Isn't this—our time together—isn't that worth a little bit of a hassle?"

Not meeting Skyler's gaze, Gaia took a healthy sip of her wine. She appeared to be contemplating his words. Finally she looked up. "You're right," she agreed. "We'll work out a story. I'm all over Brando."

Skyler beamed at her as if he'd just won the lottery. Gaia almost hated to see how satisfied her compliance seemed to make him feel. "Excellent," he enthused. "I'll get the check."

It seemed
like such a
long shot—
but then
again, **insecure**
he didn't **and**
have
any **uncertain**
shorter
shots left.

JAKE MONTONE WAS AT THE END OF

Slim to Nil

his rope.

Of course, being at the end of his rope was pretty much par for the course with his relationship with Gaia. Gaia just wasn't like other girls, to say the least. Other girls threw themselves at Jake, whereas with Gaia, Jake had practically had to chase her down to get her to agree to date him. Other girls worried about lip gloss and carbs, while Gaia studied karate and ate doughnuts like they were going out of style.

He loved it.

But lately some sort of change had come over his girlfriend, a change that wasn't exactly subtle. Where Gaia had been strong and self-sufficient, she now seemed insecure and uncertain. She was acting almost... *normal*. It wasn't fun.

And then there was Skyler.

He wasn't sure how exactly Skyler had become the white elephant in the room with him and Gaia, but somehow he had. Skyler Rodke was Gaia's new BFF, and she was practically blowing off her own boyfriend for him. This was problematic on a number of levels. The situation with Gaia was complicated.

Someone was after her. Gaia's uncle Oliver said so, and even though Gaia didn't trust Oliver, Jake did.

And while back in the day Jake wouldn't have thought that Gaia needed protecting, well—that was then, this was now. Jake was really getting off on playing hero.

So when Gaia hadn't shown up for classes that morning, Jake had gone after her. Sure, Gaia skipping out on school wasn't exactly a newsworthy event, but Jake was desperate to get through to her.

Jake's first stop was her boardinghouse on Bank Street. The chances that she'd actually be there were slim to nil. Under the best of circumstances Gaia tended to avoid the place, cramped and unpleasant as her bedroom was. She didn't love her housemates, two other children of agents who were far too accustomed to being shuttled from one locale to another, never knowing a true home. And Suko, Gaia's housemother, was practically an iron maiden. She ruled with a strong fist, and her house policies were virtually unbreakable. She wasn't especially fond of Jake, either, whom she viewed as a nuisance. So no, he didn't really expect to find Gaia at the house. But he had to start somewhere.

He pressed the doorbell and stepped back, waiting.

After a moment the door swung open inward, revealing one of Gaia's housemates, Zan.

Jake groaned. Zan was a total burnout and a flake. She also seemed to harbor a monster crush on Jake. Even if he hadn't been totally sprung on Gaia, there was no way Zan would ever be his type. He just wasn't into the streaky-dyed-blond faded-rock-star look. And though he was generally up for a party, he wasn't into hard-core drugs, which Zan clearly was.

Even at this early hour she looked much the worse for the wear. Her eyes were caked with heavy black liner that was probably left over from the night before, and her garish red lipstick had migrated beyond her lip line, to a clownish effect. To say that her hair was tousled would have been generous.

Zan's eyes widened at the sight of Jake. Her pupils were dilated, he noted. "Hey, look who's here," she said in a singsong lilt, stepping past the front door and onto the stoop. Her torn concert tee slipped off one shoulder, *Flashdance* style. Jake wasn't impressed. "Your girlfriend isn't here—though I'm sure you knew that."

Jake gritted his teeth and tried unsuccessfully to mask his annoyance. He didn't want Zan to know just how badly Gaia was dissing him—but he *did* need to know where she was. "Do you know where she is? When she left?" he asked, aiming for casual and missing it badly.

Zan shrugged, giggling. "No idea. She never came home last night. Of course, that's also old news," she said, referring to the last time Jake had come looking for Gaia only to find that she'd spent the evening with Skyler. "D'ya think she's with that other guy?" she asked mischievously.

Jake did indeed think that, which was just the

problem. He sighed and sat down on the top step of the stoop. He was back to square one, it seemed.

Zan seemed to take this as an invitation to join him. She lighted down just a few inches away, `practically in his lap.` She lowered her head to her knees. "I'm dying," she moaned. "I think I took it a little too far last night, you know what I mean?"

"Uh, maybe," Jake said, not eager to engage her in conversation.

"I know, I know—you're such a *good boy*," she said to him in a mocking tone. "But believe me, if you'd just try Invince once, you'd understand. It's a killer hangover, but is it ever worth it."

Jake didn't know and really didn't care. But he didn't have any leads on Gaia, either. "Yeah? How often do you do it?" he asked her.

"Oh, I don't know. A few times a week. If I could, I'd do it every night. It's crazy, feeling invincible like that. A perfect drug with the perfect name. Invince. . ." She repeated the name of the drug slowly, as though savoring the shape of the letters across her tongue. "It's like, no pain, no fear, no. . . nothing." She rubbed her arms and shivered with pleasure.

"Neato," Jake deadpanned, wondering why he was wasting his time with this crackhead. What help could she possibly be? `And the stoop was making his butt cold.`

"Hey," Zan said suddenly, as if a lightbulb had gone

on over her head. "You wouldn't happen to know where I could get another hit?"

Jake looked at her and shook his head. "Nope. Never tried it. But don't you have a dealer of your own?" he asked, frankly curious. Why would someone like Zan need his help to score?

She nodded. "Uh-huh. But he's a little unreliable." She laughed bitterly. "Calls himself God. What a trip. Of course, given the power he's got over me and half the city—well, maybe he *is* God. Or at least some god. Who knows? Anyway, he comes to the park a few times a week, but you can't, you know, just get in touch with him whenever you're jonesing. It's his terms or bust. Which kind of sucks."

Jake suddenly straightened where he sat, mind whirring. "God. Does he deal anything other than Invince?" he asked, careful to keep the eager hitch out of his voice.

Zan shook her head. "Don't think so. Invince's, like, his specialty. That's what he's here for. Like a, uh, *godsend.*" She snickered at her own joke and then rubbed her temples regretfully—as if the laughter had been too much for her throbbing head.

"Okay, so, uh, when did he first hit the scene?"

"Um, I guess a few weeks ago. Around the same time that people started acting whacked out on Invince," she said, sounding much more logical than usual. "Duh."

Something in Jake's mind clicked. Oliver had told

him to be on the lookout for anything new, and Invince, well. . . that was new. Was it just a coincidence that Gaia had started acting insecure and timid at around the same time that half of New York City was dosed with fake adrenaline? It seemed like a long shot—but then again, he didn't have any shorter shots left. He turned and faced Zan again, earnestly placing one hand on her shoulder.

"Zan, when are you supposed to meet God again?" he asked, hating how desperate he sounded.

Zan held his gaze for a moment, then broke into hysterical laughter, practically cackling.

"Day after tomorrow, Jake," she promised, her voice raspy from one too many cigarettes. "Day after tomorrow you can go to the park to meet God. Then you can see what it's like.

"To be fearless."

From: jakem@alloymail.com
To: gaia13@alloymail.com
Re: We need to talk

   Gaia, I really think we need to talk. We
haven't been getting along for. . . well, for a
while lately, and I think we need to do something
about it. I think it's really messed up that we
aren't going to prom together, and it's really
messed up that we haven't really spent any time
together in days. I'm sorry that you think I'm
taking Oliver's side over your own, and I'm sorry
that I just can't trust Skyler Rodke. But can't
we work past all of this? When I think about the
trouble we went through just to get together to
begin with, it makes me even more unwilling to
let it all go so easily.

   What do you think?
   ¬J

From: gaia13@alloymail.com
To: jakem@alloymail.com
Re: We need to talk

I agree, Jake. I hate the way things have been lately. I'm sorry that my life has been so complicated, and I'm sorry that once again I've dragged one of the people I care most about into it. I'll give you a call later and we can figure something out.

Thanks for hanging in,

me

He had to
give the
people
what **verboten**
they wanted.

WASHINGTON SQUARE PARK WASN'T

exactly known for its lush foliage, but there were enough trees in the park to provide adequate coverage for God's purposes. All he really needed, after all, was a sliver of shade. A sliver of shade and some willing customers.

Divine Savior

In Washington Square Park he had both in spades.

God had managed to keep demand for Invince high by using a three-pronged approach, one so simplistic that he couldn't understand why other dealers hadn't adopted it sooner.

When Invince first hit the scene, it was a mini-explosion. Tweakers, potheads, even crack fiends—everyone wanted to try the drug that made you feel invincible. Could you blame them? There was nothing else like it out there on the market. So after the drug had made a splash, once news reports starting coming back of increased violence, daredevil pranks, and the like, God knew that he'd scored. That was the first step. Getting the product out. Known. In demand.

The measured doses were his second step. Unlike the ubiquitous dime bag of weed, Invince was available only when God said it was. Which meant a couple of times a week or so. Often enough to keep the addicts panting, but not often enough for anyone to get bored or burn out.

As if one could burn out on invincibility. Ha!

His third step in securing his stronghold was equally simple: he didn't deal with the plebes. No way. God dealt with the dealers. He was, in essence, a *distributor*. He dealt to the dealers and *they* dealt to the low-life scum-of-the-earth druggies. No need to sully himself among the common folk.

So a few times a week, just as the drug-addicted populace was getting *really* antsy, God appeared on the scene, like the divine savior that his title implied. He cut a few deals with a few losers with overdeveloped senses of importance, and then he slipped back into the shadows. Quietly, discretely, without fanfare.

He knew the laws of supply and demand, after all. He was as familiar with them as he was with the laws of human nature. And his knowledge of both subject areas was what made him such a success.

That, of course, and a great product.

"Yo," a voice hissed from deeper within the shade of the scraggly tree. God whirled around to face a skinny young man whose acne-scarred face was partially obscured by a do-rag. Talk about an inflated sense of importance. What was this kid, thirteen? Probably thought he was really tough because he carried a knife or something in his pocket. Please. God could easily take him out with a sneeze.

Needless to say, God was not impressed. "Yes?" he said impatiently, letting his buyer see just how not intimidated he was.

"Yo, you got the stuff?"

"Well, of course. Wasn't that our deal? I told you I'd be here, after all." God smiled, though in the shade, his customer couldn't see him.

"Yo, so I got the cash," Dealer replied, swiftly fishing a wad of twenties from the back pocket of his oversized jeans. He held the roll toward God and flipped the edges once for good measure.

God snatched the cash out of his client's hands. He didn't care about the money. It was a nice perk, but it wasn't the point at all. He certainly wasn't going to bother to count it here, outside, in daylight. He pocketed it smoothly.

"How many tabs?" he asked quietly. "I can't quite recall."

Dealer glanced nervously over each shoulder, as if suddenly doubting his supplier. Not like they hadn't been doing business for the last two weeks—three times a week, to be exact. Please. "Yo, don't you remember? I asked for ten sheets."

"Right, of course." God nodded, smiling softly. "I should have remembered that you like to buy in bulk."

Dealer finally cracked a grin, albeit a small one. "What can I say, man? Demand is high. I gotta give the peeps what they want."

"Of course," God agreed. "That's always been my motto." From deep within his long, dark coat he produced a long roll of paper perforated into sections. He ticked off five perforations, then tore off a healthy section of the roll, presenting it to Dealer with little fanfare. Dealer hastily shoved it into his back pocket, which seemed to function as his carryall, being very careful all the while not to bend or fold the paper.

"That's always been my motto," God repeated, liking the sound of it. Dealer glanced up uncertainly, not sure whether or not he was expected to respond. Unable to think up the appropriate reply, he remained silent, readjusting the waistband of his pants now that his stash was firmly stowed.

God wasn't waiting for an answer. His gaze was already fixed on the distance, where customer number two was loping toward him, eager to make a deal. He couldn't spend too much time on any one client. Demand was high.

He had to give the people what they wanted.

From: megan21@alloymail.com
To: tammiejammie@alloymail.com
Re: Scale of 1 to are-you-joking?

Hey girl—

Just got back from shopping downtown. Found, seriously, the *cutest* pair of sandals to wear with the jeans we bought last week, no joke. And the heel's that perfect level, you know, where it's comfortable to wear but also very slimming. . . .

But I digress, big time.

The point is that who should I run into while strolling along Houston Street but Miss Moore. And I *do* mean "run into." Seriously, if I were, like, a grand master martial arts warrior like her, I might pay *slightly* closer attention to where I'm walking. But the big hulk just stepped right into me as if I wasn't even there.

And why, you may ask, was our darling Gaia so distracted? Hmmm. . . well, let's see. Two words: Skyler Rodke. As in, not Jake. As in, not her boyfriend. As in, what is *up* with that girl lately?

I am so confused. First she was mucho out, and of course—'cause she's a weirdo. But then she was a little in because, well, she had the Liz Rodke stamp of approval. Then she was out because she went behind our backs to that big Rodke society party, the be-otch. But then she was in again because she had all that *O.C.*-style angst going on with Jake et al., and we thought she was sort of pathetic and felt sort of sorry for her.

And when all is said and done, the girl still does have some sort of bizarre Midas touch when it comes to men.

I'm just confused. I mean, the hottest guys in school go after her even when she treats them like dirt. Jake Montone, the newest tall, dark stranger, could have anyone he wants. And she's *cheating*? I totally can't decide. Cool or lame-as-freaking-anything? On a scale of 1 to 10, how much do we despise Gaia Moore?

That's all I want to know.

ps: heard back from USC today—I'm in! Time to party!

From: tammiejammie@alloymail.com
To: megan21@alloymail.com
Re: Scale of 1 to are-you-joking?

You have *got* to be kidding me. Jake finds out that Gaia's running around with Skyler, somehow in some alternate strand of the time-space continuum Jake forgives her, and you find her up to her old tricks.

No way. No freaking way.

Can't decide if I'm disgusted or just plain in awe. We're gonna have to watch and wait.

ps: must see your shoes!
pps: USC—awesome! Must register for Tanning 101!

CONCENTRATING FIERCELY, GAIA LEANED

Skyler Trance

over Skyler's laptop, the glow of the computer screen illuminating her features. She closed out of the Internet and quickly entered into his system setup, deleting all of her cookies. She didn't know what Skyler was up to, but something told her he wouldn't

be pleased to discover that she'd been e-mailing Jake. Given that Skyler had pretty much coerced her into going to the prom with him instead of Jake (not that—as much as she hated to admit it—she'd needed all that much coercing) and had in essence forbidden her to call Jake or anyone else, it stood to reason that e-mail was verboten as well. But what he didn't know wouldn't hurt him.

She and Jake *did* need to talk, that was for sure. Especially now that she had somehow snapped out of her Skyler trance. She only hoped she hadn't damaged her relationship irreparably. Her relationship with Jake—like most of her relationships, come to think of it—had had a rocky start, but it was special to her. It had only been very recently that they'd agreed to give it a try as proper boyfriend and girlfriend. True, her relationship track record wasn't stellar, but even Gaia wasn't ready to throw in the towel just yet. So she was thrilled to see that he had e-mailed her, wanting to talk. And she was *going* to talk to him, just as soon as she could. Just as soon as she could get away from Skyler, that was.

Lord only knew when *that* would be.

She'd gone back to his apartment with him the night before, after they'd run into Megan. They had ordered Chinese food and rented *The Wild One*. It had been a mad Brando fest. They had read their fortunes aloud, adding the hilarious clause "in bed" to the platitudes. "Always be flexible. . . in bed." "Fortune will smile upon you. . . in bed." A laff riot. Gaia had acted docile, pleasant, and nauseatingly grateful to be in the presence of Skyler and his overwhelming generosity. She hadn't bothered to ask where the heck his roommate was or why said roommate was never, *ever* home when Gaia came over.

When it came time to go to bed, Skyler tucked Gaia into his own bed, firmly insisting that he was going to take the couch. Except for a back rub that lingered just a beat too long, he had been a perfect gentleman.

Gaia was sick of it.

Skyler had disappeared this morning on a quest for "the best bagel on campus," and Gaia had encouraged him along on his sojourn. She needed some time alone to clear her head. Checking her e-mail, connecting with the outside world. . . that was just the first step.

She was in her enemy's lair. Alone.

This was an unparalleled opportunity.

If Skyler was a threat to her, she knew—if he was an enemy worth his salt, there wouldn't be much to find in his apartment. Otherwise he'd certainly never have left her there, unguarded.

But that didn't mean she couldn't do a little digging.

THINK, GAIA COMMANDED HERSELF.

Effects of

And think fast. Opportunities don't get much more golden than this.

She scanned the perimeter of Skyler's apartment from her perch at his desk in the common area. She always marveled at how stylish it was for a college student's living space. The high-tech furniture, the unexpected details, like the heated towel racks and the Japanese screen surrounding his bed. And then there was the magazine collection perfectly fanned out on the coffee table. Nothing unusual there. . .

Not that Gaia had expected Skyler to leave a file folder labeled TOP SECRET: KEEP OUT sitting on the kitchen countertop or anything. But it would have helped.

The bathroom. You could learn a lot about someone

based on what they kept in their medicine cabinet, Gaia knew.

Skyler's cabinet was an odd juxtaposition of moldy toothbrushes, crusty tubes of toothpaste, and upscale grooming products from places like Kiehl's. Either Skyler and his roommate were total opposites when it came to hygiene, or one of them had a serious case of split personality. Either way, Skyler's/his roommate's apparent predilection for "short and sexy molding creme for hair" wasn't all that useful.

The drawer underneath the sink yielded a dried-out bottle of Los Angeles Latte nail polish by OPI. Gaia speculated as to what manicure-prone lady friend had left it behind.

Damn it! The bathroom was a bust, and Gaia had no idea how soon Skyler would be back. How long could it take to get bagels? Sure, half of the city was probably standing on line at H&H right now, which could mean a lengthy wait, but still. . . did she want to risk getting walked in on?

Her curiosity got the best of her. Gaia tentatively stepped toward Skyler's roommate's bedroom. She pushed the door open slowly, wincing a bit as the hinges creaked.

Skyler's roommate, provided that he did exist, was essentially a Spartan. The room was all but unfurnished. Pushed toward the far corner was a sad little single bed, made, but with basic army-navy variety wool blankets. Next to the bed sat a dresser that appeared to also function as a nightstand, despite being too tall to serve the task properly. And pushed against the wall next to the open door was a desk.

Gaia hesitated. Assuming that Skyler hadn't lied about having a roommate, she was engaging in a serious invasion of privacy right now. Even if Skyler was plotting against her, who was to say that his roommate was in on the game anyway? She really didn't have much justification for peeping into the desk drawers. . . yet.

She was going to anyway.

She heard the front door catch with a clicking sound that meant someone was working the lock. *Skyler.* She didn't jump or start—the benefits of being herself again—but rather retraced her steps slowly out of the bedroom, pulling the door shut behind her but keeping the image of the desk sharp in her mind's eye. Somehow she'd come back to it later. Either to rummage through it or to commit the contents of the drawers to memory. One way or another, she'd figure out what Skyler was up to. She quickly crossed to the kitchenette, digging out a bag of fresh coffee beans and pouring the specified amount into the coffee grinder. *I'm just helping out with brunch, Skyler,* Gaia thought. *Not snooping, not doing anything of note. It's all perfectly innocent around here.*

For now.

"HONEY, I'M HOME!" SKYLER CALLED in his best Ricky Ricardo voice as he crossed through the front doorway. Seeing Gaia man-handling his coffee machine, he broke into a wide grin. "Coffee! Perfect!"

Feeling Claustrophobic

"Yeah, except this machine is jammed. Seriously, don't you guys ever clean it? I mean, *you* may be down with a loose interpretation of cleanliness, but sooner or later your roommate is bound to complain, no?" Gaia asked, raising an eyebrow at Skyler.

Skyler placed the brown paper bag of bagels on the counter and came up behind Gaia. "Do you think I would live with a neat freak?" he asked her pointedly.

"Touché," she replied. Suddenly Skyler's body was very close to hers. He had lined himself up directly behind her and was now reaching his arms around her in order to fiddle with the coffee filter. Feeling claustrophobic, she ducked out from underneath him. "Great. You can deal with the toxic coffee grounds and I'll set up." She dove into the bag and dug out the deep tubs of cream cheese and lox spread, removing the lids and placing the containers on the table. "I don't suppose you got the guy to slice up a tomato for us?" she asked.

"'The guy' didn't give me a chance to ask," Skyler explained, grabbing a sharp knife and following Gaia over to the coffee table with a few butter knives and two plates. "The coffee should be ready in a moment," he said, settling down next to her on the couch.

"Excellent," Gaia answered, taking the sesame bagel Skyler offered her and buttering it thickly. She took a huge bite and chewed blissfully. This undercover work wasn't all bad news. "Mmmm," she said, savoring the chewy texture. "Perfect."

"It was worth it, wasn't it?" Skyler said. "Being separated from me for a brief hour?"

"Well, of course the emotional scars will need time to heal, but I'll forbear," Gaia deadpanned, flashing a quick grin to show that she was kidding. Sort of. "It's okay. It was good practice for later." She glanced up from her plate to see how he would react to that statement.

Skyler looked confused. "Why? What's happening later?"

"Well, I really do need to go shopping for a prom dress, Skyler," Gaia reminded him. "Especially now that I've got a new date."

Skyler smiled uneasily but recovered quickly enough. "I have it on good authority that your date thinks you look beautiful in whatever you wear," he said, winking.

"That's sweet, but come on, Skyler. It's the prom. It's supposed to be the biggest night of my high school career—sadly enough. Everyone is going to be wearing something new. I mean, even if I wanted to wear something I already had, I'm not the kind of girl who just *has* dresses lying around in my closet. You must know that." Wasn't it obvious?

The patience Skyler had exhibited the evening before had clearly dissipated. He looked decidedly unthrilled with her decision to separate from him. "Gaia, I'm sorry, but I was really hoping to spend the day together."

"Well, okay—if it's so important to you that we spend the day together, then why don't you come with me?" Gaia asked testily. *Careful,* she thought. *The sick thing is that a few days ago, you wouldn't have challenged him in any way. Skyler's wishes were your command.*

"Gaia, shopping isn't really what I had in mind for us today. Come on—I've got my masculinity to uphold."

"Right, okay, fine. The point is, I want to get a prom dress, and I don't see why you're making such a big deal about it," Gaia said flatly.

"Gaia, I think you're being a bit unreasonable. For the past week or so I've been here for you, practically at your beck and call, taking care of you, giving you whatever you need. I don't understand why suddenly you can't trust me to know what's best."

Gaia had run out of plausible protests, so she resorted to pouting. Unfortunately, he made a very logical argument. Seeing as how she'd basi-cally lost her mind for the past few days, it was hard to justify suddenly coming to her senses without arousing suspicion.

"Look, I have to go out for a bit."

So that was why he didn't want to go shopping. He had other plans. Which was pretty unusual. Suspect, even. Until now, whenever Gaia was around, the only plans Skyler had revolved around her.

"What for?" Gaia asked.

"I have an errand to run. I'm sorry, but it can't wait. You should stay here. I don't want you getting into any more random scrapes or anything, okay? I'll be back, and then we can go see a movie or something. Even go shopping for prom dresses if you're absolutely set on it." A week ago she wouldn't have thought twice about obeying Skyler's directive. The idea made her shudder.

Well, if Skyler was going out on a so-called errand, the proverbial lamb was sure to follow.

Has anyone seen my friend formerly known as Gaia? Or, I guess, if you want to go for accuracy, my Gaia formerly known as my friend? Yeah, I know the drill—you want hang with Gaia, you've gotta be willing to penetrate her steely exterior (or at least withstand it, you know?) and just let her various overwhelming intimacy issues roll off your back. And—oh!—you can't assume you'll see her in school because, you know, she doesn't really attend with any great regularity. And you can't think that she'll return your calls in a timely fashion. Sometimes there's a good reason for this. Sometimes there's a great reason for this. Sometimes there's a reason that one never becomes privy to. Go figure.

So, okay, any friendship with Gaia Moore comes with a lengthy warning label. But I've read the fine print, and I thought we'd made some sort of progress. I mean, maybe we weren't going to be huddling around any campfires singing "Kumbaya" anytime soon, but you know—we cared about each other in our own ways. Gaia's way was complicated and enigmatic. My own? Not so much. I basically worshiped the ground she walked on (still do, to be perfectly honest). But it was an understanding, and it was mutual.

Maybe I blew our one shot at true romance all on my own. Maybe my jealousy was a large part of what caused us to self-destruct. True, I couldn't stand to see her with Sam Moon. For some reason I just couldn't trust that the two of them were *just friends*. Possibly because any boy in his right mind who has the exquisite pain-wrapped-in-pleasure of encountering Gaia Moore is sure to fall in love with her. It's like some weird male death wish or something. But I digress.

The girl has been completely gone as of late. She came to see me in the hospital the other day,

babbling something about how it
was all her fault that I was in
there in the first place; then
she freaked about boyfriend trou-
bles (always fun to hear about),
and then. . . well, then she disappeared.

And though I haven't seen her
since, I've been *hearing* all
sorts of weirdness to do with
Miss Gaia. Like that she's been
spending the majority of her
time with Skyler Rodke, for
example. Which is, okay, not
exactly "alert-the-authorities,"
code-red-style behavior, but
random nonetheless.

It's possible I'm overreacting. Maybe Skyler's A-OK, and he
and Gaia are, in fact, huddled
around the aforementioned camp-
fire singing "Kumbaya." Maybe
she's happy as a clam up in his
apartment, watching movies, eating pizza, drinking beer (I'm
just going on my basic assump-
tion of college-type activities). Maybe he's really a
friend to her, and once again my

own Gaia meter prevents me from
being objective. Maybe.

But I don't think so.

So if you do see her? Yeah,
can you let her know I'm looking
for her? That'd be groovy.

If there *was*
a "way" to
go about
this, **alternate**
which
he was **universe**
starting to
doubt.

JAKE SCANNED WASHINGTON SQUARE

God Is Dead, Man

Park tensely, trying to determine where to begin his quest to find God. Any of the various losers draped across the park benches surrounding the fountain could have the information Jake was looking for. Conversely, they might not even know their own names right now. It was a crapshoot. If only Zan had given him more to go on. Of course, getting anything useful out of that girl was a miracle in itself. Which was cool. Jake was down with the smaller miracles, the day-to-day kind. Some hope was always better than no hope, no matter how you sliced it.

Jake decided to start small. He inched his way toward a slim, wiry young girl with a mop of dirty-blond dreadlocks tied loosely at the nape of her neck. She wore a T-shirt over a long-sleeved thermal, even though it was at least seventy-five degrees outside, and appeared to be squinting from behind darkly tinted sunglasses. Her olive green cargoes were fraying at the hem. She sat cross-legged on the bench closest to Jake, clutching a jumbled mass of keys held together on a giant plastic ring.

"Hey," Jake said softly. She looked like she could possibly be asleep sitting up, and he didn't think waking her abruptly was the way to go about this. If there *was* a "way" to go about this, which he was starting to doubt. "Um, nice keys. You must be able to get in, like, anywhere," he ad-libbed.

The girl tilted her head up toward him, derision etched across her features. Jake thought it was pretty interesting that a key-obsessed freak who appeared to spend the better part of the day on a park bench should be treating him with condescension. But then again, he needed her way more than she needed him. "Whatever," she whispered, further driving the point home.

"Do you hang out here a lot?" Jake asked. As he said it, he realized that he sounded like he was hitting on her in some weird, druggy, alternate universe. *Whoops.* "What I mean is," he went on hastily, "what I mean is that I'm looking for someone who hangs out here a lot, and I thought you might know him."

"Who?" she asked, her curiosity obviously getting the better of her persistent suspicion.

"God," Jake said, suddenly feeling immensely foolish.

She snorted and went back to her key ring. "God is dead, man," she said. "Everybody knows that."

Jake contemplated her words momentarily. "Fair enough," he said, shuffling off. No reason to waste further time with her. But who next? He had skipped out of third period for this once he'd realized that Gaia was blowing off school yet again. At least this way he didn't have to explain his undercover action to her. The thought was of small comfort. He was doing this *for* her, after all, and he hated to think that she couldn't be in on it or appreciate it. "Later," Oliver had promised him, "you can be Gaia's knight in shining armor later, when we've gotten to the bottom of this." But later seemed very far away.

Jake's gaze fixed on a large African American man squatting next to a small tree, swathed in layer upon layer of ratty blanket. A supermarket shopping cart was perched next to him. Unlike the dreadlock girl, this guy was definitely more likely a long-term resident of the park. Jake decided to try his luck.

"Hey there," he said easily. "I'm looking for a friend of mine. He hangs out here sometimes. Do you hang out here a lot? Maybe you've seen him."

"It only rains in purple on Tuesdays," the man said, smiling a soft, dazed smile. "Banana."

O-kay. "Banana?" Jake repeated questioningly, feeling ridiculous.

"The caterpillars eat banana," the man clarified proudly.

Jake had a feeling that this bit of random science trivia was completely false, but he wasn't about to argue the point. "Sure," he agreed affably, moving off.

Strike two.

A bluish arm flopping down from a bench suggested life beneath the paper bags strewn above it. Feeling impatient by now, Jake marched over and prodded the arm with his foot. "Excuse me, can I ask you a question?" he began loudly.

He was met with a distinct lack of movement from beneath the paper bag covering.

Visions of police chalk outlines running through his head, Jake backed off quickly. *Strike three*, he decided, dejected. *Now what?*

"Day after tomorrow, six a.m.," a voice whispered in his ear suddenly. "That's when God comes," the voice hissed.

Jake whirled around. He was greeted with the visual equivalent of the hissing voice, a lithe, slinky, shirtless man covered in tattoos.

"How do you know?" Jake asked, trying to keep his voice from shaking.

"I know you're looking for him 'cause I heard you ask that cute little coed over there," the man said, jerking his thumb toward the bench, where Dread was now waving her fingertips in front of her face, a glazed look in her eyes. "I know he's coming 'cause *I'm* waiting for him, too."

"God, you mean? You're sure we're looking for the same guy?" Jake asked, barely allowing himself to believe that this man could have the information he was looking for.

"Oh, sure. God. He only comes a few times a week. Not regular at all. And never the same time twice. Likes to keep us all guessing. Playing God, you know." At this, he broke out into a phlegmy cough that sent Jake back a few paces. "He'll be here tomorrow at six."

"Six in the morning?" Jake confirmed. He wasn't sure how willing he was to deal with God in the park at six in the morning, even if that wasn't the most macho thing to admit.

"Yuh-huh. Then you can get your hit of invincibility," the man said, his lips stretching across his teeth to reveal one capped gold and one rotted, stripped away to a vile shade of mottled gray. Jake shivered.

"But you know, he only deals with the top dogs," the man continued. "No amateurs looking to score dime bags of weed," he scoffed.

"Yeah, I know," Jake said, trying to infuse his voice with more tough guy than he was feeling. What was wrong with him? He'd faced way worse than this with Gaia. At the very least, he could handle this freak show, who looked like he hadn't eaten in days. "So thanks, man, for the lead. I've been looking for this guy for a while. I'll be here tomorrow."

"Sure," the man said simply. He pursed his lips together as if deep in concentration. He leaned in toward Jake, who paused, tense.

"I AM GOD!!!" the man shouted at the top of his

61

lungs. Spittle sprayed across Jake's cheeks. Reflexively he pushed the man off him.

"Whatever, dude," the man said angrily. He hooked his hands into his jeans pockets and strode off, frustrated.

Freak Show had been his best bet, his top lead, the only one who really seemed to know what Jake was talking about. But that had been before his raving-loony outburst. Now what? Did that make his claims less believable? *Big fat DUH*, Jake decided.

But he was going to have to come back tomorrow anyway. Pretend to be a "top guy" drug dealer or something. Tomorrow at six. Based on little more than the ramblings of a crazy man.

Because right now, the ramblings of a crazy man were all he had to go on.

Here we go again.

I don't know why I'm surprised anymore. The routine is so established, I could recite it in my sleep: Get abandoned (in one form or another) by the people that I love. Try to get by on my own. Meet someone new who somehow manages to crack my overriding suspicions and worm their way into my good graces. Develop a rapport with said new person. Become vaguely dependent on said person, at least to the extent that I grow to expect him or her to be around.

Discover that the person in question is, in one way or another, out to get me.

Good times.

Granted, I was not in top form when I met Skyler Rodke: I was reeling from the aftereffects of serving as Dr. Rodke's little science project. (Voluntarily, no less. Yeesh.) So okay, the whole "getting to know someone and slowly coming to trust them" was

GAIA

a bit compromised. Clearly I
wasn't using, uh, my best judgment. But still. . .

Just once, couldn't someone be
a genuine friend?

Oh, I know there've been people in my life who haven't had an
agenda or an ulterior motive.
Like Sam, or Ed, or Mary. People
who cared about me and, inexpli-
cably, just wanted to be with me.

Yeah, those were the people
who got shot, or killed, or otherwise hunted down in the
streets.

Welcome to my life.

So here I am, stomach filled
with gourmet bagels and OJ,
creeping down an uptown street,
flattening myself against building walls at the slightest indication that Skyler is going to
turn around and spot me. I
promised him I'd stay in his
apartment. He didn't disbelieve
me when I told him so. He's that
used to me taking his orders at
face value. But a perfect pattern
is destined to repeat itself ad

infinitum, and like everyone else, Skyler is out to betray me.

I follow at close range—ten paces behind. My worn-in sneakers are soundless against the asphalt, my drab, peeled-from-the-floor-of-my-closet ensemble does nothing to set me apart from any other pedestrian up here—I could pass for any other nondescript student or dropout. When he turns, I turn; when he crosses the street, I cross the street; when he pauses, I duck down and hold my breath. But he doesn't know that I'm following him. Because I've gotten very, very good at this.

I've had to.

And you know what the kicker is? In the whole miserable time since my uncle betrayed my father and we relocated to the Berkshires—in the face of everything that's happened since then—I've given up any sort of expectations of having a normal life. I mean, please. I'm not a moron. I can recognize a sealed

fate when it hits me over the
head. But somehow, somewhere, in
the furthest recesses of my
heart, I guess I really am a
sucker. Because although I no
longer harbor expectations of a
normal life, there's still a part
of me that hopes for. . .

No, I can't. It's too ridiculous.
But. . . nonetheless, there it is—
I still hope for a happy ending.

I never was much for fairy tales. Maybe it was a guy thing, but the whole "happily ever after" always struck me as seriously fake. Me? I prefer a good action movie, where the muscle-bound hero bursts through the door packing high-octane explosives, taking down any bad guy who dares to get in his way.

Happy endings are for losers.

When I first met Gaia, I expected her to be just like all the other good-looking girls I've encountered in my life—shallow, vain, and most of all, interested in me.

I couldn't have had it more wrong. When I first met Gaia Moore, she couldn't have been less interested in me. Which, to be honest, was a little bit baffling. But also refreshing. It was nice to be the pursuer for the first time ever, nice to feel like I had to expend a little effort.

And once I got to know Gaia,

it became obvious why she couldn't be bothered to spend all day in front of the mirror, brushing her hair or putting on another coat of lip gloss or whatever it is that girls do when guys aren't around. Gaia had bigger fish to fry.

Going to Siberia with her was a major trip (no pun intended—ha ha). Whatever bad blood is between her father and her uncle, it isn't going to be healed overnight. The stakes were high over there—we weren't just playing at action heroes: we *were* action heroes. Just like when I helped Gaia to escape from that fake loony bin out in Fort Meyers, Florida.

I know Gaia hates her life sometimes, and I guess I can understand why, but I gotta tell you—to me, it's less of a burden and more of an adventure. I do care about Gaia, and sure, I wish that all of this excitement weren't at the expense of her happiness and her stability, but even with those caveats. . .

It's a pretty freakin' good time.

Take this afternoon, digging around in the park, questioning all the freaks and weirdos about the great and powerful "God." Most guys I know talk tough but wouldn't have the balls to walk up to random psychos and strike up a conversation. But I can. I've had practice. I'm coming up under the best. Gaia can say what she wants about her uncle "Loki," but he's taken me under his wing and shown me some amazing things. He's turned me into some kind of James Bond, something bigger than any of the dorks from my old dojo could possibly appreciate.

It sucks that all of these spy games are somehow at Gaia's expense. It sucks that she feels so put upon, that she can't enjoy these experiences. I don't like to feel guilty while I dig around behind her back, damaging whatever trust may still remain between us.

It sucks, yeah. But you know what?

I'm not going to stop anytime
soon.

I can hear what you're thinking. I know you probably think
I'm a liar, untrustworthy, insen-
sitive to my girlfriend's feelings, yadda, yadda, yadda. You
might be right. But that doesn't
change anything. Because when all
is said and done, like I said—I'm
having a hell of a good time
these days.

And in the process I just
might be saving Gaia's life.

Memo

From: C
To: L
Re: J

   J was spotted in Washington Square Park,
inquiring about a drug supplier, code name "God."
Expressed intention to return tomorrow at 6 A.M.
to meet with God. Follow him?

Memo

From: L
To: C
Re: J

    J is not a threat. He is not to be harmed.
However, you are encouraged to continue your
surveillance. Report back promptly as new developments unfold.

which was always a good time

sticky metal bin

GAIA PRESSED HERSELF AGAINST THE
wall of the dank alleyway, not
daring to breathe. Given that she
was cuddled up next to a
Dumpster that was giving off a
not-so-fresh scent, this was
probably for the best. On the
other side of the Dumpster, Skyler
was on the phone. She had no
idea who he was talking to. But he
was arranging a meeting.

Up Close and Personal

She had followed him to a very sketchy back alley
on 121st Street, no less, where Columbia University
buildings slowly gave way to housing projects and
shady-looking storefronts. Skyler had ducked off of
Amsterdam Avenue, and Gaia had flattened herself
against the front of the building, where there was no
possible way for him to see her. She kept a sharp eye
out but didn't see anyone else go into the alley, which
seemed odd to her. She crept into the alley and saw
that Skyler was partially obscured by the huge, smelly
Dumpster. And so she had sidled on up to the opposite end of it, listening.

Then she heard Skyler speaking, and it became
clear—he was making a phone call. A phone call
that, for some reason, he wasn't willing to make at home.

"It's me," she heard him say loudly. Though he

didn't identify himself by name, he made no effort to disguise his voice. For a few moments all was quiet. Gaia physically ached to hear what the person on the other end of the line was saying. More than anything, she longed to race at Skyler and pin him down, demanding to know why. Why he had suddenly become one of the many people who were out to screw her, what he had to gain, who his allies were. It was a physical reaction; she had to exert fierce concentration to prevent herself from rushing forward and giving herself away. *Why?* she thought, the blood pounding in her temples.

After what felt like hours but in reality must have been mere moments, Skyler spoke again. "I see," he said tersely. "Aha. Okay. Well, I suppose we'll have to meet," he said brusquely, the voice of authority. Gaia's ears perked up. *Meet?* Another opportunity for her to do some recon. Another opportunity to follow and perhaps, with any luck, uncover. This was good. This was information she could use. This was an opportunity to take an active role in defeating Skyler at his own game—before he could bring her down.

Another pause, then, "Right—Bowery and Bleecker. Northwest corner. Number 45 Bleecker, room 314."

Corner of Bowery and Bleecker, Gaia repeated to herself, fishing a ratty-looking pencil from the depths of her messenger bag and hastily scribbling the address on the back of a gum wrapper she'd found.

Sure, she had a photographic memory and all, but this was no time to take chances. *45. Nwst corner.*

"One-thirty. Not tomorrow. Day after. Right," Skyler finished. Gaia dutifully jotted down the time. Her ballpoint pen cut waxy trails in the paper, but it worked. "I'll be there," Skyler promised his mystery contact.

Gaia shivered. *So will I,* she promised silently. *So will I.*

"Yeah," he said gruffly. "I heard you." He paused, listening. "Back at the apartment. I promise," he answered to an unknown query. Then, "She has no idea."

She has some idea, loser, Gaia thought angrily. *And she's gonna take you down, that's for sure.* 45 Bleecker. That was easy. She'd be there. But for what? What was Skyler up to?

As if in response, he spoke again. "Later. She's at the apartment, waiting for me. But I'm gonna head to Queens for a while. . . . Easy, take the 1/9 down to Forty-second Street and switch over to the N/R." Pause. "I know, I know, but I don't think I'll be able to get there faster. A cab will take too long. There's always bridge and tunnel traffic. It's no big." He laughed shortly. "Trust me, she'll stay put. Yes, even if I'm gone awhile. *Trust me,*" he insisted, "she won't even blink."

Gaia heard a quick beep as his phone clicked off. Thinking fast, she dropped soundlessly to her knees and then to her stomach. As she imagined that Skyler was dropping his phone back into his jacket pocket, she slid on her stomach underneath the Dumpster. That way he wouldn't see her when he turned to leave the alleyway. Also, she could get up close and personal with the underside of the bin. Which was always a good time.

Grimly determined, she breathed through her mouth and squirmed underneath the sticky metal bin. It was a small price to pay, she reasoned, for getting to the bottom of Skyler's bull.

That, and getting even.

GAIA STEPPED INTO SKYLER'S

Ultimate Warriors

apartment and deposited her MetroCard—the one she'd used to jimmy his front lock open—on the kitchen counter. The front of her sweatshirt was caked with sticky Dumpster grime, and suspiciously tinted flecks of some unidentifiable substance clung to the tips of her ponytail. But at least her efforts hadn't been in vain. She knew where Skyler was—that was to say, out somewhere in Queens—and that he wasn't coming back until much later. She knew he thought that he could pretty much stay out as long as he needed to and that she'd basically be waiting for him whenever he returned.

He was sort of right.

In two days she'd be at 45 Bleecker at Bowery, ears open, ready for some insight on just what the hell Skyler, his father, and God only knew who else were into. For that matter, if she really put her mind to it, she could even manage to squeeze in a long-overdue heart-to-heart with Jake before Skyler came home.

And if she was really efficient and really, really careful, she could do some classic ransacking.

She had every indication that Skyler was working against her. She was banking on the fact that she'd seen him hit the subway toward Forty-second Street, where she knew he wanted to catch the train to Queens. She knew he would be out for a while longer running his messed-up *le homme* Nikita head games. So she'd come back to his place to check out his roommate's room again more thoroughly. There was something hidden in that room, she knew.

She entered the room and slid open one of the lower desk drawers. Out popped a file cabinet, manila folders crammed tightly in place. Gaia crouched down to read their labels. GENE SPLICING, one read. *Um, okay.* Safe to say that at the very least, Skyler was using his roommate's cabinets to store his own files. EFFECTS OF, read the folder just behind it. Barely daring to hold her breath, Gaia had reached her fingers in to pry the folder out when suddenly she stopped dead in her tracks.

MILITARY USE.

Military use? Military use of what? Military use of fear? Military use of lack of fear?

Gaia's throat felt tight and closed, and her breath came more sharply now. Her uncle, Oliver/Loki, had once harbored designs of replicating Gaia's fear-suppressed DNA to create an army of ultimate warriors. . . . That hadn't really worked out for him. His fear serum had yielded tragic side effects, from shaking, to blindness, to—in some cases, when left unchecked—death. So Gaia had just assumed that once Loki had been foiled, the idea of removing fear from soldiers in combat had finally been dismissed.

She knew, now, never to assume again.

GAIA BREATHLESSLY PUSHED OPEN

Exhibit A the door to the Starbucks on Sixth Avenue, doing a quick scan of the room to see if Jake had arrived yet. It was four-fifteen, which was exactly the time they had agreed to meet. Gaia had never been one for punctuality. But with all of the secrecy, distrust, and miscommunication between her and Jake lately, she figured it really couldn't hurt to be on time.

Clearly, though, Jake didn't share her opinion.

Not that he was technically late yet, of course. And he probably wasn't expecting her to be shockingly prompt. Little did he know that she was supercharged from the findings of her recent recon mission. Supercharged? Scratch that—she was ready to burst out of her skin.

The coffee shop was humming with a quiet level of energy, about half filled, mainly with spillover NYU students either on their way to or just coming from class. Gaia ordered herself a cup of coffee, milk and sugar—no four-dollar designer drink for her, thank you very much—and collapsed at one of the unoccupied tables toward the front of the coffee shop, near the door.

She was nervous for Jake to arrive, nervous as to what they were going to say to each other. She wasn't ready for their relationship to be over—it hardly seemed like it had even had time to get off the ground—but it certainly looked like things were headed that way. And that sucked. There were so few people in her life that Gaia felt she could depend on, she really wanted to be right about Jake.

"Sorry I'm late," she heard from a voice above her,

just as someone leaned in close and kissed her on the cheek. "Were you waiting long?"

And there he was. Gaia couldn't help but take a moment to check him out. He looked great: fresh from a shower and clean smelling, with his thick hair tumbling down over one eye. He pulled out the chair opposite Gaia and sat down to face her.

"No, I just got here," she replied quietly, feeling suddenly shy. "It's good to see you."

"It's good to see you, too," Jake said warmly. Dimples erupted in either cheek, and Gaia felt a fresh wave of embarrassment that she had ever blown him off in favor of the seriously disturbed Skyler.

"So how come you weren't in school today?" Jake asked.

"Wait," Gaia interrupted. "It's nothing, I promise— but—did you hear from any schools yet?" Like most seniors at the Village School, Jake was waiting on his college acceptances. No matter what else was going on, Gaia did have some basic understanding of normal high school priorities. She wanted to know how he was doing.

Jake grinned again. "Yeah. Got into Northwestern and BU. My dad's crazy overexcited about it, like I just got married or something. But I'm still waiting to hear from some others." Jake knew better than to throw the question back at Gaia. To say she was private—and unconventional—was the understatement of the century. He wouldn't have been surprised if Gaia were to go into paramilitary training after graduating from the Village School. "Now answer my question."

Gaia couldn't possibly tell him that she had spent the day with Skyler. He wouldn't understand why Skyler had suddenly become her best friend, and she could now finally see why he thought it was weird. Frankly, she couldn't believe it had taken her so long. Sure, in a perfect world, her boyfriend would trust that her friendship with another male was purely platonic, but. . . Then again, when it came to her bizarre relationship with Skyler, she couldn't blame him. She obviously didn't trust it herself. "Um, I had a headache when I woke up and just decided to blow off school."

"Like you ever need an excuse," Jake said, laughing.

"Yeah, true. But this time I had one. Then later on, when I was feeling better, I decided to go shopping for a prom dress." Gaia gave a sideways glance at Jake to see how he reacted to the words *prom dress*. Jake knew that Skyler had offered to go to the prom with Gaia. And he also knew that Gaia had accepted the invitation. Which was, effectively, exhibit A in the evidence of their ruined relationship.

"Did you find anything?" Jake asked, frank curiosity etched across his handsome features. If he was sad about the fact that they weren't going to prom together, he wasn't showing it. Gaia was going to have to pry it out of him.

"No, I didn't. Which really sucks. You know me—I hate to shop. I *so* do not want to have to go back again later on, but I guess I do."

"Well, yeah, I guess you do," Jake agreed. "Unless you want to go to the prom naked, which—hey, no arguments here."

Gaia couldn't help but laugh. "Pervert."

"What?" Jake protested. "If I can't go as your date, you leave me with no options. Cheap thrills are all I'll have left. Don't rob me of those, Gaia."

Still laughing, Gaia decided to go for broke. *What have I got to lose?* she wondered. "Well, I won't go naked," she said solemnly. "But maybe I can cut you a deal."

"What sort of a deal?" Jake teased, trying to keep things lighthearted. "Careful—my virgin ears can't take anything more risqué than a PG-13 rating."

"Don't be gross," Gaia said, more earnestly now. "I'm trying to talk to you seriously."

"Okay," Jake said. He seemed to get that she wanted to have a real conversation. He sat up straighter in his chair. "I am all about your deal. Deal me, Gaia. Hit me."

Gaia sighed. "Jake, I have no idea how things got so messed up between us. I mean, wasn't it just like last week that we were having another conversation, saying that we were going to try to be boyfriend and girlfriend?"

Jake nodded. "Yeah, it was. That meant something to me. And I thought it meant something to you, too. Gaia, I don't get what you're playing at. Going to the prom with Skyler, hiding out from me, skipping school without any warning or any notice, calling me every five minutes and then refusing to return any of my calls. . . What's up with that?"

Gaia shook her head sadly. "I know, Jake. I've been weird and bipolar lately. I wish I had a good excuse for it, but I don't."

"Is it because I wouldn't side with you against Oliver?" Jake asked softly.

Gaia stirred her coffee aimlessly with a soggy wooden stirrer. She wasn't sure how to answer that question. Yes, it irritated her endlessly that Jake wouldn't take her word for it that Oliver was evil. But then again, why should he? There were some things that people just had to learn for themselves. "Well, I mean, yeah, that bugged me. Just because I know him better than you do, and I know what he's capable of," she added hastily. "I mean, I do wish you could just take me at my word, but I get that you need to have your own relationship with him. I guess it's cool that you can form your own opinion of him. And you know, with any luck, you won't ever have to see the side of him that I saw. So no, that's not a big deal."

"I am sorry that you think I've been behaving suspiciously," Jake said. "I know it creeped you out when you found me in your bedroom at the boardinghouse. The only reason I was camping out was because I really wanted to talk to you and I hadn't been able to get in touch with you. I was *worried* about you. But I didn't mean to invade your privacy, and I certainly won't do anything like that again."

Gaia smiled. "I appreciate that. And I get why you did it, and I really don't hold that against you. Heck, I might have done the same thing if I were in your shoes. For my part, I didn't mean to go MIA. I really think there was something wrong with my phone or whatever. You're not the only one who told me they'd been trying to get in touch." *Something wrong with my phone?* she wondered silently. *Or someone?* Would Skyler have tampered with her phone? It seemed unlikely, but at this point she knew better than to discount any possibilities.

"Hey, these things happen," Jake said, letting her off the hook as she had done for him. "The question is, where do we stand now?"

"That's the question," Gaia parroted, suddenly losing her nerve.

Jake reached across the table and tenderly took her hand. "Gaia, I was thrilled when you said that you wanted us to be together. I know I pretended to give you a hard time, but the truth is that there was no doubt in my mind it was worth a shot. And I don't think we've given this a fair chance. I guess the question is, do you?"

"No," Gaia said simply, meeting Jake's gaze head-on. "No, I don't."

"Well, then, for chrissake, *why* are we behaving this way?" he demanded, grinning to take the sting out of his words.

"'Cause we're losers?" Gaia offered.

"Hey!" Jake exclaimed. "Speak for yourself."

"Okay, *I'm* a loser," Gaia clarified.

"Watch it," Jake warned, caressing her cheek with his hand. "That's my girlfriend you're talking about."

Gaia blushed. "I promise, Jake—no more games," she said. "And I think we should go to the prom together. I don't know what alternate reality I was visiting when I told Skyler I would go with him, but I was obviously having a manic moment."

Jake snapped his fingers in mock disappointment. "Damn," he said.

"What?" Gaia asked warily.

"I guess I'll have to tell Tammie Deegan I can't go with her." The twinkle in his eye belied any truth to his statement.

"You are *not* going to the prom with Tammie!" Gaia shrieked, knowing as she said it that of course it wasn't happening.

"True, I'm not," Jake said. He took her hand in his own again. "I'm going with my girlfriend," he clarified. "That is, if she'll still have me."

"I'll ask her," Gaia assured him.

Jake let her comment go and leaned in for a quick kiss, sealing the deal. "No more games for me, either," he said. "I promise."

And in the moment, Gaia believed that he meant it. Almost.

From: C
To: L
Re: J

   Subject spotted with Genesis, having coffee.
No further information is available at this time.

Memo

From: L
To: C
Re: J

Please stop wasting my time.

Just when, exactly, did I relinquish control of my own life, huh? Was it when I readily signed my free will over to Skyler Rodke? Earlier? When I allowed Dr. Rodke to instill fear in my sensory-deprived system? 'Cause I swear, it's been ages since I've been the boss of me.

Jake says that he's looking out for me, that he just wants what's best for me. He says he'll be wary of Loki, and I understand that some things just need to be learned the hard way. But still. What it comes down to is this: Jake doesn't trust me when it comes to Oliver. Jake thinks he has a better handle on the guy than I do. I can just sense it.

But Jake is wrong. And that's a lesson he can't *afford* to learn the hard way. Not if his life depends on it. Which, in my personal experience, it just may.

Jake wants to be with me, to get back together with me and do all the WB-style teen-angst rela-

tionship things with me. And the
disturbing thing is that that's
what I want, too. Despite all that
I've encountered, I still haven't
learned my lesson. I'm still holding out for that happy ending
where I go to the prom with my
boyfriend wearing the same stupid
dress as my best friend. I want it
so badly that I'm willing to over-
look the obvious.

I think Jake might still be in
bed with Loki.

(Not like that—get your mind
out of the gutter. Big fat ewww.)

It's no secret that he really
got off on the double-oh action of
our Siberian rescue mission, and
he rose to the occasion when I was
trapped down in Florida. But the
thing is that to Jake, this is all
a game. Fun and games, and my dear
uncle Oliver is the ringmaster.
What he doesn't get is that Oliver
is no ringmaster.

More like a puppetmaster. And
Jake could be his shiny new
marionette.

So Loki thinks there's some

new threat on the scene, someone out to get me. Well, if it's Tuesday, someone's after Gaia. Yawn. And sure, maybe this time it took me a while, but I'm finally on to it. Thank God. So I don't need Loki's help. Like the saying goes, *With friends like him.* . .

Good thing I don't really have any friends, huh?

Loki's right—there is someone after me. But I don't want him and Jake doing my dirty work for me. For one thing, when Loki gets involved, I can't always tell whose side he's on. But more than that, I just can't risk Jake getting hurt. He just doesn't get it. He doesn't get that this is real life. This isn't some video game that you can reset to start over when you wipe out. If this goes badly, he could wind up. . . Well, I don't even want to go there. Game over. For yet another of the people who matter most to me.

He doesn't care. He's too accustomed to the dojo or to

organized, disciplined, orderly
sports. Games. Games where
there's a ref who blows a whis-
tle when things get screwed up.
To him, this alliance with Loki
is like the ultimate three-point
shot: a chance to be the
ultimate hero.

And the chance is worth so
much to him that he's willing to
betray me. To lie to me. To vio-
late my trust. Or so I think.
Suspect. Fear.

And I'm letting him.

I'm so far gone, so twisted,
that some part of me still
responds to him. God help me, I
want to believe him when he says,
"No more games," even though I
know I can't. I was right about
Skyler, I've been right about
Loki time and time again. If I
have a hunch about Jake, well. . .
I just might be right about him,
too. I have to assume that he's
reporting back to Loki after our
every conversation. I have to
assume he's keeping tabs. For the
time being, I have to consider

the possibility that my boyfriend is my enemy.

I should hate him, I know. How can a girl still care about someone who so clearly doesn't have her interests at heart? Or rather is so misguided in what he thinks my interests are that he just may endanger us both? How can I just sit back and allow this?

I don't hate him, though. I don't hate him at all. I may have gotten *Alias* instead of *90210,* but I still can't bring myself to hate him. Who knows? Maybe if I hold out long enough, I'll somehow regain control.

Maybe, if I keep my wits about me, I can write my own script. One where Oliver is gone and Jake is on my side.

Maybe, just once, I can have my happy ending.

I've been thinking a lot about comic book superheroes. You know—Bruce Banner, Peter Parker, Clark Kent. . . They all had one thing in common. (Well, two things, I guess, if you're counting the fact that they all have these nifty alliterative names.)

Duality.

Each of these heroes had mild-mannered aliases that they assumed by the light of day. Each had a secret that he couldn't share with those closest to him. Each fought tirelessly for the greater good but under the "guise" of his true identity and couldn't take any credit for his actions. Each was forced to create the persona of an average, everyday human being.

I know how that goes.

I mean, not to say that I'm like Superman or something. I don't believe in magic, and I don't think I'm larger than life. I know people think I'm cocky, and maybe I am, but there's a

FAKE

limit. No, I'm not larger than life. But I am involved in something larger than myself.

It's hard, though. It's harder than I would have thought, this duality, double life. . . duplicity. Because no matter how often I tell myself that everything I do, I do for Gaia, the fact is that it *is* duplicitous. It is a deception. I sat across the table from my girlfriend and I told her that I wouldn't play any more games.

In effect, it wasn't a lie, I guess. I mean, to me, this isn't a game. Oliver tells me that there's someone after Gaia, and if Gaia isn't going to let him in to trust him again, then I am going to have to step up.

It's not a game, but it's not really the truth, either. I'm basically working against Gaia. Against her wishes, alongside her uncle. But what she doesn't understand—what I don't think she'll *ever* understand—is that by working with her uncle, against

her wishes, that's *exactly* how
I'm working *for* her!

See? Duplicity. Duality.
Irony.

And Gaia thinks I don't pay
attention in Conroy's English
class.

But it's not about literary
devices or tricky semantics. As I
said before, it's about comic
book politics. Superman loved
Lois Lane, but he couldn't reveal
to her his true identity (well, I
mean, he did, but then he had to
go back in time and erase her
memory and it was that whole
thing—not really the point). So,
effectively, he lived his life
deceiving the woman he loved. For
the greater good. Because he had
to. A lie for the greater good is
just a white lie, right? "The
ends justify the means"? Who said
that?

Oh, right. Machiavelli.

Not such a superhero after
all.

The truth of
what Ed
was saying
was so
obvious
as to
completely
escape her.

the elusive blond

LIZ RODKE WALKED DOWN THE HALLWAYS

Gaia-Related Frowning

of the Village School more slowly than usual. She was looking for Gaia, who—big shock—didn't seem to be at school. Of course, as near as Liz could tell, Gaia seemed to view the whole school thing as optional. Or at least, she operated on a schedule of flextime. Which, Liz supposed, was vaguely cool, especially since Gaia was some sort of quasi genius who evidently didn't need the same education that the rest of the common folk did. Though her teachers weren't necessarily in on the scheme. . .

Whatever. Liz shook her head, frustrated. The point was, Gaia was nowhere to be found. Which was really a shame, for two reasons:

1. Gaia was one of the only cool people to be found at the Village School and definitely one of the only girls that Liz could stand.

2. Gaia had been acting erratic and jittery lately—not at all like her usual badass self—and Liz was a little worried about her.

She took a right turn outside the science lab and sidled up to Gaia's locker. Sure enough, Gaia wasn't there. Liz discovered, however, that she wasn't the only one searching for the elusive blond. As Liz rounded the corner, she saw a slightly disheveled Ed Fargo staring blankly at Gaia's locker door, as if he'd forgotten why he stopped by in the first place. Liz didn't know Ed all that well, but through Gaia she'd learned that he recently had been cured of a massive skateboarding injury that had left him paralyzed. Under normal circumstances, it was easy to imagine Ed as a skate rat daredevil: he was a typical class clown, self-deprecating and always up for a laugh. Liz rarely saw him frowning, as he was now. But she was given to understand that most of his frowning was Gaia-related. Ed had dated Gaia for a while before Liz came to New York. Liz didn't know exactly why it had ended, but she knew that right now, their relationship was a little strained. Yet here Ed was, staring at Gaia's locker as though if he concentrated hard enough, he could create her from thin air just by the sheer force of his will.

"Hey," Liz said, offering a tentative smile and a wave. "You haven't seen her either?"

Ed started out of his reverie and looked up, blinking. "Huh? No," he confirmed. He shook his head emphatically, as if clearing away his mental cobwebs. "God, sorry. I don't know where the hell I just went. I was trying to remember the last time I'd seen or spoken to her, and I blanked out. I wanted to see what was up with her, maybe find out if she'd heard from any colleges." He paused thoughtfully. "If she applied to any colleges."

Liz laughed. "So I'm guessing it wasn't that recent, huh? The last time you saw her, I mean."

"Well, a few days ago. But since then she's been incommunicado. Which I guess I should be used to," Ed said, sounding resigned but not angry.

"Yeah, I get the feeling that Gaia can be hard to pin down," Liz agreed. "But I wanted to talk to her. She seemed upset the other day, so now that she hasn't been in school. . . I don't know, I guess I'm being like a nervous mother or something. I mean, Gaia can take care of herself."

"Well, yes and no," Ed hedged.

Liz didn't quite want to ask what he meant by that. "I guess, you know, if you see her—let her know I was looking. And I'll do the same for you," she suggested.

"Sure," Ed said, snapping back into full consciousness as if by the flip of a light switch. "If all else fails, we'll see her at prom, right?"

"Yeah, definitely. I mean, are you. . . You guys aren't going together, are you?" Liz asked. She would have thought that Gaia would be going with Jake since they were technically together. But she hadn't seen them hanging out over the last few days, and the last time they spoke, Gaia told her that Jake hadn't asked her yet. So really, it was anybody's guess.

"Oh, no," Ed replied. "I'm taking Kai. I mean, even though we aren't dating anymore, she's really cool and fun, and we both thought we'd have a good time together."

"Yeah, you definitely will," Liz affirmed. From what she knew of Kai, she was bubbly, sweet, and very easygoing—a perfect platonic date for someone like Ed.

"I thought Gaia would be going with Jake," Ed continued, echoing Liz's thoughts. "But when we talked about it, she seemed weird."

"I'm not sure when he asked her," Liz filled in. "I think she was nervous about that. Which, I mean, is totally ridiculous. Obviously Jake asked her."

"Well, yeah. . ." Ed trailed off, looking uncomfortable.

"What?" Liz demanded.

"It's just that then I heard a *really* strange rumor. Normally I would just, you know, consider the source and completely blow it off, but. . ."

Liz's eyes narrowed with suspicion. She fixed Ed with a scrutinizing gaze. "Spill it, Fargo," she insisted.

"Listen, I heard this from Megan, who. . . well, anyway, I heard it from Megan. But I heard. . . I heard that Gaia was going to the prom with your brother," Ed finished awkwardly.

Liz's forehead creased in confusion. At first she didn't get it. Gaia and Chris were friendly enough, but—well, Chris was gay, and if he was going to go the "take-a-friend" route, he had closer friends than Gaia Moore. The truth of what Ed was saying was so obvious as to completely escape her. Realization dawned in her mind just as Ed offered clarification.

"I heard she was going with *Skyler*."

LIZ FOUND HER BROTHER CHRIS

Against All Laws of God and Nature

studying in the library, perched at a large wooden table surrounded by chemistry textbooks. He looked deep in thought, but she was undaunted. She marched up to him purposefully, her blond hair trailing behind her like in a power shot from *Charlie's Angels* or the latest John Woo movie.

"What the hell?" Liz demanded, grabbing Chris's arm roughly and yanking him around so he was facing her. Several students hovering nearby looked up in mild alarm, suggesting that maybe her tone was a few octaves higher than library decorum dictated. She didn't much care.

"Um, excuse me?" Chris asked, looking extremely annoyed. "I have not the faintest idea what could possibly have your panties in a bunch, so for the love of Pete, please clarify."

Liz had the decency to look slightly abashed over her physical assault. Nonetheless, she was too stunned by Ed's recent revelation to be distracted from the matter at hand. "Did you *hear* who Gaia is going to the prom with?!"

"Uh, no, but my guess is that you did, and for some reason, it's a match you deem against all laws of God and nature, huh?" Chris quipped wryly. "Fill me in, sis. The suspense is killing us." He gestured grandly to the small audience Liz's histrionics had amassed. A gaggle of FOHs, led by Laura, were openly staring. Liz stared Laura down until she had the decency to look away. *Gossip-hungry jackals,* she thought fleetingly. She looked up again to find Laura eyeing her new T-shirt with the cute flutter sleeves and subtly adjusted her posture so as to really give the trend-seeking fashion victim a better view. *As if she'd ever have an original stylish impulse of her own,* she thought, knowing she was more irritated by the weirdness going on between Gaia and Skyler than anything else.

"She's going with *Skyler,*" Liz hissed fervently.

Chris's eyes darkened momentarily. He composed himself quickly—but not quickly enough to escape Liz's notice. "See?" she said. "You think it's weird, too!"

"Why would I care who Gaia goes to the prom with, Liz?" Chris asked, with as much derision as he could muster. "She's *your* friend."

"Okay, first of all," Liz said excitedly, lowering herself into the seat next to Chris and leaning forward with urgency, "she's your friend, too, so don't try to be all too cool for school, okay? And second, he's your brother, so you have to have at least a little bit of interest in that. And third. . . well, *ick*! I mean, he's *Skyler*. . . . He's our brother. . . . He's. . ." She trailed off, floundering. Just why *was* this bothering her so much, anyway? Was it because she was *jealous*? No, she wasn't petty that way. It wasn't so much that Skyler was stealing her friend so much as. . . the *way* he was doing it. College guys dated high school girls all the time, so it wasn't the age difference. And she honestly wouldn't have cared if Skyler and Gaia were involved. But she knew, as much as she could possibly know, that Gaia was totally hooked on Jake. Which made Gaia's relationship with Skyler a little creepy. And the way that they always seemed to be disappearing together. . . And why was Chris being so normal about this? Since when was he such a paragon of maturity? He *hated* Skyler, even though he would have denied it if she asked.

"Don't you think it's odd that every time she drops out of sight, it turns out she was with him?" she prodded. After all, it had to bother Jake.

What was she thinking? She knew for a *fact* that it

bothered Jake—he had practically threatened her the other day, coming by their house and demanding to know where Skyler lived so that he could go get Gaia away from there. Clearly Jake also thought this whole business was a bit strange, which emboldened Liz to stick to her theory.

"What I think is weird is that you're so obsessed with what's going on with them," Chris grumbled. "I mean, jeez, so what if she *is* playing around behind Jake's back? What's it to you?"

Liz shrugged. She couldn't articulate it well enough. Chris was right—her reaction was strangely visceral. She really *didn't* care who Skyler dated. But the fact was, she couldn't shake the nagging feeling that something about Skyler and Gaia's dynamic wasn't completely kosher. Not to mention, Gaia hadn't been herself lately. Could it all be related? "I. . . don't know," she said finally. "I guess maybe you're right. Maybe it's nothing."

"I didn't say it was nothing," Chris interjected testily. "I said, it's nothing that interests *me*. And that I'm not really sure why you should care. I know she's your friend, but it's not like he's talked her into bank robbing or something like that. For all we know, they've been hanging out at his apartment lately—so freaking what? If there's something up, ask her. If you're such close friends as you seem to think you are, she'll tell you, right?" Chris paused, looking self-righteous. "I don't know what it is about that guy, but he makes the strangest choices," he muttered, almost to himself. "Yet he always manages to come out smelling like a rose."

There it was—the competitive edge that she'd come to expect. "Um, having a momentary attack of sibling rivalry, are we?" Liz asked. She had no idea why Chris always got like this. It was true: Skyler *was* something of a golden boy—off at Columbia, ready to work at their father's business. He was good-looking, poised, and charming. But then, so was Chris. It was as though Chris had some sort of bug up his butt about their brother—like he almost *wanted* to create a competition that wasn't there. In fact, just about the only thing that Skyler had "over" Chris was that he was the oldest. But that was just a technicality, right?

"You said it yourself—you think he's messing with your friend," Chris continued. "Doesn't that piss you off even the slightest? He's gotten under her skin and may or may not be undermining her relationship with her boyfriend. And you don't even have any control over the situation." Angry red blotches stood out on his cheeks. Liz realized that he was getting pretty r i l e d u p . *Abort mission, abort mission,* she thought. Chris had way too many issues with their brother to be a helpful ally in this situation. If she *was* worried about Gaia, then she was going to have to intervene on her own.

"It *does* piss me off—that's what I was trying to tell you," she reminded him gently. "But you're right—I'm probably overreacting. I'm sure I'll feel better once I've had a chance to talk to Gaia. Forget I said anything. I'm sorry I bothered you."

"Whatever," Chris snapped.

Liz pushed her chair back from the table, acutely aware of the dull scrape that her chair made against the floor. Now that she'd calmed down a little, she felt more worried than ever—that her fears were founded. But there was a more grounded, rational bent to her anxiety. Ironically, she preferred the blind, misguided panic. It was a more insistent emotion, but one that was easier to dismiss as mere dramatics.

As she slung her bag over her shoulder, she noticed again that she and her brother had gathered quite an audience. The FOHs, now slack jawed, still regarded her. Tammie caught Liz staring and smirked at her knowingly. Liz didn't dignify the behavior with a reaction. She had bigger concerns. For now, she had to find Gaia.

What's the deal with sibling rivalry? Is it something that's genetically hard-wired? Biologically programmed? A Darwinian imperative?

No, really. Inquiring mind wants to know. 'Cause for my part, I just don't get it.

Of course, it's different for me. Not only am I the baby of the family, but I'm the only girl. So basically I was alternately taunted and coddled by both of my brothers and—let's be real now—pretty much spoiled by my parents, God bless 'em. I've got no cause to complain, to be sure.

But if you're going to play that game, then, well, neither does Chris. Yet. . .

Maybe it's unavoidable, something we're all prone to. After all, the first documented case of sibling rivalry goes way back to the first volume of the good book, suggesting that it's inherent to the human condition. I mean, look at Cain and Abel:

Competition for their father's
affection (even if it was only
perceived competition) was so
acute that one killed the other.
(Cain. Cain killed Abel. I think.
I never went in much for reli-
gion. Always very distracted by
the cute boys in Sunday school
class. But anyway, one of them
was killed by the other. Which is
all kinds of messed up, if you
ask me.) And then of course there
were Jacob and Esau and later on
Joseph, who was sold into *slavery*
by his brothers.

Yeah, I guess sibling rivalry
is a pretty whacked-out, powerful
emotion.

Other than the mere, very basic
fact of being brothers, Chris and
Skyler have no reason to compete.
They couldn't be more different
from each other. Skyler is suave
and charming where Chris is ener-
getic, sharp, and cynical in a
very funny way. For that reason,
both are great to have at parties. Both are very smart, though
Skyler is more of a diligent

worker whereas Chris has the "mad genius" thing going—he either excels or flunks, depending on his level of interaction with the material. Not that it matters. He's doing well enough at Village School, and he'll go to a good college. I hate to admit it, but some lower grades in some lame lit classes just don't matter that much when your father's been listed in *Fortune* as many times as ours has. Sick, but true.

Both are great looking, Skyler with his soap-opera eyes and Chris with the all-American-boy appeal. Neither has ever lacked for his share of suitors. And that, too, was never a point of contention for them, of course, since Chris came out so early on.

For that matter, Chris's sexual orientation was never a big thing for any of us. Thankfully, he was self-aware enough to recognize that he was gay, so there wasn't a lot of tortured confusion (well, no more than the usual adolescent angst, anyway).

And my parents really took it in stride. They may have been surprised at first, but they're open-minded and very loving. I don't want to speak for him, but I think what could have been a difficult time for Chris was actually pretty painless.

And the future? Well, again: hate us if you need to, but the future is pretty damn bright for all three Rodkes. My father is a keen businessman, that much is clear. And he chose to go into a business that, as I see it, won't ever go out of style. Women aren't ever going to stop needing cosmetics. Are you kidding me? Once upon a time, little girls wore Barbie lip gloss. Here in New York City they're going for weekly manicures and getting their faces done at Barney's before birthday parties, no joke. Again, sick but true. We've got role models like Madonna and Susan Sarandon—women who are way more gorgeous in their forties and fifties than I might hope to be in my twenties. And suddenly the bar is that much higher. And Rodke and Simon? Well, it's like the holy grail: one of the most powerful international pharmaceutical companies, leading the way in drug research and development in addition to all of those amazing skin-care products and makeup and stuff. My father's company has the edge on some impressive medical advances. For obvious reasons. And we're all set.

My parents don't play favorites. I think I'm pretty objective, and that's the truth as I see it. I've been told since I was old enough to understand that there's room for all of us in the company business. So there's no reason to feel like any one of us is going to be edged out.

But maybe that's where the sibling rivalry, alpha male thing comes in. Maybe there has to be *one* true leader. I don't like to think about it, but eventually my father won't be around to head the business. Myself, I'd be perfectly

content to be an active partner.
Or who even knows? Maybe I'll do
something else entirely. But
that's just it. That might be the
missing piece. *Someone's* going to
have to have to step up to take
the mantle. To be president. And
while it could be worked out equi-
tably—a partnership? I'm not a
corporate shark—maybe this is
where survival of the fittest
comes in. Maybe when it comes to
brothers, there is no equity.
Maybe it's like a biological,
physiological, psychological
thing. Maybe it's something my
brothers can't avoid, even if they
wanted to. And maybe—I think *probably*—it's dangerous.

Maybe, at the end of the day,
someone's going to have to come
out on top.

GAIA SAT NERVOUSLY, HER FEET

Not Afraid

propped up on Skyler's coffee table in what she hoped was a casual manner. He would be home any minute now, she assumed, and she had to pull herself together before he was. She grabbed at a magazine and flipped through it idly, realizing a beat too late that she had it upside down. *Get it together, Gaia,* she chided herself. She couldn't allow any indication that she had followed him before, that she had been out with Jake. . . or that she had come back to his apartment to ransack it in his absence.

So here she was, just a few hours later, sitting nervously on his couch with her feet propped up in a relaxed pose. The pose was a sham. Gaia was anything but relaxed. She almost couldn't believe that all of her suspicions about Skyler had proven to be true. Although come to think of it, nearly everyone in her life had disappointed her at one point or another, so she didn't know why she should be so terribly surprised.

Okay, Skyler, she thought with grim determination, *two can play at that game. You like surprises? Well, I've got one for you. However I may have behaved before, I'm back.*

I'm back, and I'm not afraid of you.

Gaia heard the lock click in Skyler's front door and

steadied herself for his return. Her blood was literally boiling from all she'd uncovered, but she couldn't let Skyler see any difference in her demeanor. *At last,* she thought. She was glad that true to his word (though not, of course, his word to her), Skyler had been out all day. She assumed he'd been in Queens. But who knew? All of her assumptions about him had clearly been false. Anyway, the time alone had given her a chance to do some more rifling through the files she'd found and to copy down key phrases. Words like *gene splicing* and *adrenal suppressor*. Words that suggested someone was playing Frankenstein, planning to create a cadre of government-issued Gaia monsters.

She glanced down at the magazine in her lap. *Maxim*—three months out of date. She had it right-side up, but what was the likelihood Skyler would actually think she was reading that for pleasure? *Unlikely,* she decided. She'd left her schoolbooks at home, so she couldn't turn to those. She was hopelessly behind in English anyway. She grabbed at the television remote control and flicked it on. Keanu Reeves and Al Pacino were involved in complicated verbal banter in *The Devil's Advocate*. Gaia only recognized it because it had been on TNT just about once a night for the past month—also a testament to exactly how much time she had been spending zonked out on Skyler's couch.

"Hey," Skyler said, walking into the apartment and tossing his keys onto the kitchen counter. "Whatcha watching?"

"Three guesses," Gaia said, struggling to keep her voice light. As the signs continued to indicate that Skyler was working against her, Gaia found herself increasingly angry at this most recent violation of trust. *Normal, Gaia,* she reminded herself. *Be normal.*

"Hmmm. . . ," Skyler said, pretending to think it over. He glanced at the screen. "Okay, Al Pacino in a suit. Keanu Reeves in a suit. Panoramic skylines of New York City." He smiled with familiarity. "Could it possibly be *The Devil's Advocate*?"

"Thank God for TNT's new classics," Gaia said dryly. "I think *The Shawshank Redemption* is next." She actually liked *Shawshank.*

"Ooh, love the new classics," Skyler agreed. "But sometimes you've gotta stick to the diehards."

"*Die Hard?*" Gaia asked, confused.

Skyler laughed and crossed over to where she sat on the couch. "No, silly," he teased, ruffling her hair. "Diehards. As in honest-to-God classics. As in, we must be schooled."

"Let me guess. You brought me *Annie Hall*," Gaia said.

"Close. Sorry I'm so late. I was stocking up on provisions for our afternoon together." He grinned, mock-sheepish. "Well, more like evening now. Sorry it took me so long to get home. Hope you weren't bored."

Gaia shrugged, hoping that she looked noncommittal, but inwardly she flinched. It was slowly occurring to her that she and Skyler spent an awful lot of time on his couch. Sure, he took her out, but the unspoken rule was that she wasn't "allowed" out on her own. It was almost like she was being held hostage. As if he needed to have constant tabs on her and didn't trust her to be out and about on her own.

Creepy.

Get it together, she reminded herself again. She forced a bright smile and tried to adopt a neutral gaze. "Awesome! What'd you bring?" she said, wincing again at the sound of the word *awesome.* Who was she, some Prada-toting Friend of Heather's? *Ugh.*

"The obvious fixings," Skyler said, unpacking his grocery bag onto the coffee table. "We've got graham crackers, we've got Nutella, we've got peanut butter, and we've got Marshmallow Fluff."

"I think you've got the four food groups covered." Gaia laughed, somewhat delighted despite herself. If she had to go undercover, at least she'd eat well. "Carbs, sugar, fat. . . and sugar."

"You said 'sugar' twice," Skyler pointed out.

"I did. It doesn't matter, I'm really into sugar," Gaia assured him. "Now, what were you saying about classic cinema?"

"Voilà," Skyler said, brandishing a DVD and presenting it to her like a bouquet of flowers. "We shall pick up just exactly where our formal education left off."

Gaia glanced down at the cover of the box. *The Godfather, Part II.* Of course. "Excellent. And I suppose when this is done, we'll watch part three?"

"Well, now, that's a question," Skyler said, play-thoughtful. "You see, *Godfather II* is considered by many—though not me—to be superior to the original. Part three, however, is universally considered to be dreck. However, in the interest of being complete, we may have to watch it anyway. We can play it by ear."

"Sure," Gaia said. "I'm all for playing by ear."

Skyler grinned at her and popped the DVD into the player. Instantly Keanu's face faded to blue, and the screen was filled with the now-familiar image of the FBI warning. Gaia settled back into her usual position, secure under his arm. It was difficult to pretend that she felt relaxed, but she knew she had to try. Maybe Skyler thought he had her fooled. He couldn't have known that Gaia was no amateur. She had learned from the best—steadfast, whip-smart agents like her father and calculating rogues like her uncle or her foster parents. Please. College-boy Rodke was no match for her. She shook his arm off her back and leaned forward, breaking off a hunk of graham cracker and dipping it back and forth in each of the various jars Skyler had unscrewed. *Mmmm,* she thought, her anger temporarily replaced by a flash of junk-food sugar rush. She might gain twenty pounds figuring out Skyler's game. It was a small price to pay.

Because it wouldn't be long now.

Unfortunately,
he didn't have
the **moping**
faintest
idea how **around**
to do that.

Memo

From: C
To: L
Re: The evidence

    I regret to report that re: evidence, we have
none. Can confirm that Rodkes (aka Rodke and
Simon Pharmaceuticals) are interested in subject
Genesis's DNA, as found within hair sample. Must
assume DNA to be used in drug research and development as per recent genetic tampering on subject
Genesis.

    High probability that research related to
antianxietal development; however, to what purpose? More field surveillance necessary. Also,
without concrete evidence cannot proceed with
countermeasures. Please advise at your earliest
convenience.

Memo

From: L
To: C
Re: The evidence

Your suspicions are correct: the likelihood is
that Rodke and Simon Pharmaceuticals has designs
on creating antianxietal. Hence much interest in
the unique DNA of subject Genesis and its response
to external stimuli and manipulation. However, you
are correct—we need hard, fast proof.

Right now your orders are simple: You are to
continue your surveillance. I will do some digging. Unfortunately, for right now the boy is
still our best hope. He can get in where we might
otherwise be stonewalled. Keep in close contact.

I'll be watching Rodke, the boy, Genesis.

And I'll be watching you, too.

THE RED SOLID BALL INCHED SMOOTHLY toward the corner pocket, rolling along with quiet momentum, suffusing Ed with a false sense of confidence. *There. That's it,* he encouraged the ball mentally. *This game's all mine.*

Random Acts of Disappearance

Without warning, though, the ball veered wildly off to the right. *No, no, it's okay, I can still take this,* Ed thought, gripping the wooden edges of the pool table and leaning his entire body in the opposite direction of the ball's trajectory. *It's not over till it's—*

With a loud clanking sound the ball in question banged directly into the eight ball, sending the eight ball shooting straight into the left side pocket. The eight ball landed in the pocket's netting with a dull thudding sound.

Right.

"Whoo-hoo!" Kai hooted, pumping her arms in the air in an impromptu victory dance. "Winner and still champion!" She laid her pool cue up on the rack against the wall and hugged Ed to show that she was teasing. Sort of.

"Just remember who helped you perfect your game," Ed grumbled.

"The student hath surpassed the teacher," Kai said

formally, sounding like a cross between a Zen master and an Elizabethan page. "Ha ha," she added tauntingly, as a mischievous afterthought. She stuck out her tongue.

"Hey," Ed protested. "Can't you go easy on me? I'm still in recuperation mode. Cut a guy some slack."

"Uh-uh," Kai insisted. "You were the one who *swore* you were back in the blush of full health. You were the one who challenged me. And I might also point out that you seemed rather overconfident about the whole darn thing." She winked at him. "So there."

"This failure is very, very bad for my ego," Ed joked. His ego wasn't in especially bad shape these days.

"Ah, but your loss is my brilliant success, so in that sense, everyone's a winner. 'Everyone,' of course, being me," Kai pointed out. She giggled and hugged him again. "I'm just kidding, Ed. But you know, no one likes a sore loser."

"I am *not* a sore loser," Ed countered. Kai raised a quizzical eyebrow at him.

"Okay, maybe slightly sore. Bruised. I'm a bruised loser," he conceded. "I gotta tell you, though—being out of the hospital? Yeah, it pretty much rocks."

"I'll bet," Kai agreed.

"If I can go for, let's say, two consecutive months without, you know, needing some life-altering surgery or being attacked in a park, that'd be a huge plus," Ed said. He wasn't especially trying to be funny, though.

His life had gotten complicated over the course of the last year, and while he wasn't interested in assigning blame, there was one person who seemed, time and time again, to somehow be involved.

Gaia.

It didn't matter that Gaia was not only not interested in Ed but that lately she didn't even seem particularly keen on maintaining the most minimal level of friendship with him. He was used to Gaia's random acts of disappearance. But she always surfaced *eventually*. Lately, though. . . well, she hadn't been herself. In fact, the last few times he had seen her, she'd even been crying. Crying was distinctly un-Gaia-like behavior, and Ed wasn't sure how to contend with it. He supposed it corresponded to their no-bullshit policy, but that didn't make it any easier to deal with.

Anyway, in the time since Gaia had come to the Village School, Ed had somehow managed to have his heart broken, to be chased by various men with guns, to see his ex-girlfriend knifed in the park, to endure a dangerous operation that had restored the use of his legs, and. . . uh, he'd had his heart broken some more. And that was just the tip of the proverbial iceberg. So yeah, he was ready for a month or two of pure, brain-dribbling-out-your-nose peace and mind-numbingly boring quiet.

"Check. One normal life, coming up," Kai said,

breaking into Ed's thoughts and nearly reading his mind at the same time.

Ed managed a small smile, but suddenly he was distracted.

"Luke, I sense a disturbance in the Force," Kai said in a robotic tone. Either the girl was a psychic or he was being wildly transparent, Ed decided. He suspected a little of both.

He sighed. "You're gonna kill me."

"Um, okay. Let me guess," Kai said. "Gaia?"

Ed shrugged. *Bingo.* "I know. I'm a broken record. A lame, pathetic broken record." Not only that, but he was a *lucky* broken record—lucky that Kai was cool enough to want to be friends with him and to put up with his moping around, even though they had just broken up themselves. He certainly didn't take her for granted. "Yeah, I guess. Who knows?"

Kai wasn't buying it. "Maybe, or. . . ," she prompted. She hung Ed's pool cue up and led him over to some comfy couches off to the side of the room. "Tell me."

"Well, I don't know. I feel like all this weird stuff went down while I was in the hospital. And now I'm out, and it's great, but. . . I feel really out of the loop. Like I woke up and it was Opposite Day." Ed stopped, unsure of how to explain what he was feeling.

Kai looked at him closely. She seemed to be weighing whether or not to say something.

"Kai, speak. There's something on your mind."

She shrugged. "It's probably nothing."

"Well, if it's nothing, then you don't have to worry about telling me, right?" Ed reasoned. "You've obviously heard something, but you don't think you should tell me."

"I don't know," she hedged. "I hardly know Gaia."

"But. . ."

"Well, you said yourself she's been acting differently."

"Yeah, that's definitely true," Ed said, thinking back to her spontaneous crying jag in the hospital, where she'd told him she was worried about what to wear to the prom. "I mean, she's Gaia—she's never, you know, sparklingly normal. But lately she's been really jumpy and insecure."

"Right," Kai said, turning Ed's words over in her mind. "Right."

"But you obviously know differently," Ed prodded.

"Well, I've heard some stuff, but you know—not from anyone reliable," she started.

"Yes!" Ed agreed. He himself had heard that Gaia was going to the prom with Skyler Rodke. Sure, he'd heard it from the FOHs, who were pretty much known as Gaia's arch-nemeses (at least, they were thusly known on non-opposite days), but still. . . it was almost so far-fetched as to be necessarily the truth.

"Anyway, I know you think she's been weird lately, but from what I've heard, she's being her usual self.

You know, tough as nails, doesn't give a rat's ass. . ." Kai clearly couldn't decide whether or not she was the bearer of bad news.

"Ah, the Gaia I know and love," Ed said. He was trying to lighten the mood, but even as he said the words, he knew them to be true. It didn't matter how erratic her behavior was or how drastically she tried to push people away—Ed would always care for Gaia. That was just an absolute truth.

"Yeah. Normal Gaia. Except I heard. . . that she's been cheating on Jake," Kai finished, looking guilty. "Now I know no matter what people say about her that she's one of your best friends—"

"Most of the time," Ed interjected.

"Whatever. The point is, you care about her, and you respect her, and I respect *that*. I mean, I know you, and I trust your judgment. So if you think that Gaia isn't the cheating type, I believe you."

Ed blushed. Not too long ago, he had accused Gaia of cheating on him with her ex-boyfriend Sam. He realized now that even if she and Sam had harbored lingering feelings for each other, Gaia wasn't untrustworthy. He knew it had been his insecurities that had motivated his accusations, and the memory of the things he'd said to her still stung. "No, she definitely isn't," he confirmed.

"Right. So I just assumed they were cheesy rumors. Besides—what do I care? I mean, the only reason I even paid any attention was because she's your friend, and I know how much you care about her."

"I appreciate that," Ed said softly.

"But then I heard that she was going to the prom with Skyler! I mean, Ed, I certainly don't care who Gaia dates. But if she *is* going to prom with Skyler, then I think you may be on to something with your 'something's up' theory. Don't you think that's a little strange?" She bit her lip. "Okay, I've said my piece. If you think I'm overstepping my boundaries, you can feel free to ignore everything I've said. But if you think maybe I'm right and something is up. . . well, do with the information what you will."

Ed regarded Kai somberly but didn't reply. Something *was* up with Gaia, and he had to get to the bottom of it.

Unfortunately, he didn't have the faintest idea of how to do that. But he'd have to figure it out before too long.

From: shred@alloymail.com
To: gaia13@alloymail.com
Re: Back in the day

As in, remember when we used to be friends?
Where've you been, G?

Hey—I'm used to you dropping off the face of
the planet now and then, but that doesn't mean I
like it. Or, truth be told, that I don't worry
(yeah, yeah, I know you could eat me for break-
fast and that me worrying about you is like the
joke of the century, but there it is. . .).

I haven't seen you since the hospital, and
even though you're not exactly Little Miss
Sunshine under the best of circumstances, you
seemed pretty down that day. So if you have a
moment, I would love to hear back from you.
Seriously, no joke. I don't mean to be melodra-
matic, but you know I'm here. We don't even have
to talk about whatever's got you upset. We can
just joke around and consume massive quantities
of junk food. Or not. Whatever you want. I just
want you to know that I'm here.

And I'd love to know where you are.

—Ed

JAKE BOUNCED NERVOUSLY BACK AND
forth in his seat. The aluminum bleachers were cold and unyielding through the seat of his jeans. And he was stunned to find that he had arrived at the meeting point *before Oliver*. This was unprecedented. True, Jake was twenty minutes early, which was also unprecedented.

Whacked-Out Possibilities

But whenever he'd met Oliver in the past, he always arrived to find the man firmly rooted in the location of choice, looking like he'd been there for hours.

Today they were meeting at the ball field of the Carmine Recreation Center, a stripped-down sort of YMCA, if there was such a thing. An after-school league was in the midst of practice, and Jake enjoyed watching the small boys step up behind home plate. It reminded him of his childhood, when he'd played on almost every kiddie league his school or town offered. He'd excelled at just about every sport he tried his hand at. The boy at bat now wasn't faring so well. He looked sweaty and uncomfortable, and his grip on the bat was all wrong. Jake could tell the kid was afraid of the ball. Not uncommon, but something he'd have to get over if he wanted to be any good. Of course, as a child, Jake's only interest in the talent of the other players had been in relation to whether or not they were slowing him down.

Jake's entire body was humming with excitement. He couldn't wait to tell Oliver about his new theory. About God. How cool would it be if Jake's hunch turned out to be right? Oliver would have to acknowledge him then, admit that Jake was more than just a dumb kid. He'd have to concede that Jake was a possible protégé, someone to potentially be reckoned with. Freakin' awesome.

"You're early," a voice commented dryly off to Jake's right. Jake turned to find Oliver standing at the edge of the bleachers, looking so un-Oliver that it took Jake a moment to recognize him. Sure, he supposed Oliver intended to blend in, given their surroundings, but still... he'd never seen the man, generally given to tailored three-piece suits and carrying honest-to-God cloth handkerchiefs... Well, he'd never seen the man in *jeans*. Jeans and a T-shirt. *Will wonders never cease?* Jake thought, admiring Oliver's constant—and constantly successful—efforts to play the part to the hilt.

"Yeah, well, I finished up some errands earlier than I expected, so I figured, why not," Jake replied, smiling.

Oliver didn't smile back. "Have you uncovered any new information?" he asked.

It was hard for Jake to take Oliver seriously from behind the huge Ray-Bans he wore, but he persevered. "Actually," he began, struggling to keep his tone casual, "I had a thought."

Oliver raised an eyebrow—this Jake could see even

133

behind the oversized lenses. "Please do share it with me," he said.

"Well, okay. So I went over to the boardinghouse today to see Gaia—I've been keeping an eye on her like you said," Jake explained.

"Yes," Oliver said, waving Jake on impatiently.

"She wasn't there, but her housemate Zan was. Now, Zan's a total freak—also, I think she might have a crush on me," Jake couldn't help but add. "She does *a lot* of drugs—at least, it seems that way. So I don't know how totally trustworthy she is. But she's really into this new drug called Invince. You know, the drug that supposedly makes you feel invincible. It's the next big thing underground, I guess. People are taking these tabs, they're called Oranges, and the trip, it like makes you feel immortal. That's why there's been that huge wave of daredevil crimes. Lots of violence and stuff. Because people just aren't afraid of anything anymore."

Oliver stared coolly at Jake but didn't say anything. He kept his hands planted firmly in his pockets.

"So, okay, it got me thinking. Whoever is after Gaia stole some of her hair. Which is, you know, totally weird. But maybe it makes sense when you think about it in connection to Invince. You know—maybe whoever is creating Invince is sort of researching ways to re-create the feeling of being invincible? Refining the drug? And maybe Gaia's DNA is the key? I know its a little farfetched. But maybe they think her super-strength, super-intelligence, super-all-around-abilities are encoded in her genes? I mean, what else would they want her *hair* for? Unless whoever took her hair is just some crazed serial killer looking for a prize."

"But we know who took her hair," Oliver pointed out. "Or at least, we suspect we do."

"Right," Jake agreed, excited. Now that he was voicing it out loud, he was really warming to his theory. "The Rodkes. As in *Rodke Pharmaceuticals*. I think they're into some. . . I don't know. . . drug research or something. I mean, it's possible, right? Anything's possible? Compared to all the whacked-out possibilities, this one makes the most sense. . . doesn't it. . . ?" He trailed off uncertainly. Oliver wasn't saying anything, which was never an especially good sign. "Well, you told me to explore every possibility," he finished defensively. "So I am."

"So you are," Oliver agreed. "It's good that you did. It's important for us, in a situation with so few real leads, that we open our minds and, as they say, 'think outside the box.'"

"That's all I'm doing," Jake said, trying to sound less petulant than he felt.

"Well, that's certainly true. Have you developed any further theories?" Oliver asked.

After being shot down so quickly, Jake was loath to put forth his ideas about God, but he'd learned early on that it was best to be up front with Oliver. After all, anything he tried to keep a secret always came out later anyway. "Well, there's this dealer. He calls himself 'God.'"

Oliver gave a short laugh as if thoroughly amused by the notion.

"And he's, like, the only person who has access to Invince. He's the main supplier, and he only works with the dealers—he won't sell directly to the junkies. Anyway, I did some digging in Washington Square, and he's supposed to be there tomorrow. Or at least, that's the word on the street. I don't know how reliable the drug addicts are, but then again—you have to figure they want their fix. So I'm going to go by tomorrow, see what I can figure out."

Oliver shrugged, completely noncommittal. "It certainly couldn't hurt. Truth be told, it's a tenuous connection at best and a long shot. But by all means, Jake, go. Go and seek out this 'God.' See what he has to say."

"Yeah?" Jake asked uncertainly. He couldn't make heads or tails of Oliver's lack of enthusiasm.

"Absolutely. You're right: we don't have any better leads right now, and as long as you're willing and able, we should certainly follow those that we do have. If that means talking to this so-called God"— and here Oliver couldn't resist another derisive snort—"then that's what you should do. Go talk to him. And then come to me.

"And tell me everything."

He was
nothing if
especially
nostalgic
not an
opportunist.

From: tammiejammie@alloymail.com
To: laura@alloymail.com
Re: Caught in the act

   Well, looks like we're *not* the only ones who
think Gaia's new friendship is totally bizarro.
Good to know little miss never-fazed Liz is actually bothered by it. Makes me feel like this
nasty little rumor we've sent out into the ether
might have some bite to it—not necessary, of
course, but an added bonus.

From: laura@alloymail.com
To: tammiejammie@alloymail.com
Re: Does this mean Jake's available?

   Can I say, *yum*?!

OLIVER LINGERED AT THE REC CENTER for a while after Jake had left. He wasn't especially nostalgic by nature—well, most of the time he wasn't, anyway—but he enjoyed watching the young boys play. He could recall being that age and being sick and helpless. He remembered the seething

Nothing If Not an Opportunist

envy he had felt toward his brother as a child, his brother, the wonder boy, the one to whom everything came so easily. Even Gaia's mother, Katia. *Especially* Gaia's mother. Was it any wonder Oliver felt so protective toward Gaia? She was all that he had, all that his brother had borne that was at all accessible to Oliver. And while she certainly didn't trust him right now, he would win her back. He'd win back her loyalty.

After all, he was nothing if not an opportunist. And there was metaphorical gold to be mined from her DNA.

"Does the boy have a lead?" came a low voice from behind Oliver.

Without turning around, Oliver replied. "I'm not sure," he growled from the corner of his mouth. No use in putting all of his cards on the table so early in the game—leverage was imperative. His agents needed to be kept on their toes, information doled out on a "need to know" basis only. "It's something we'll have to keep on top of to be sure."

"He's off to see 'God' in Washington Square?" the agent said uncertainly, stating the obvious.

"Indeed. If you were listening to our conversation at all—which for your sake I greatly hope you were—then you would know that. You shouldn't need me to repeat it."

"Of course not, sir," the agent replied, sounding nervous. Loki could feel the embarrassment radiating off the man in waves. *Good,* he thought. *Humble is good.*

"Never mind," he replied curtly. "Just see that you follow Jake. I want exhaustive reports on all of his efforts—I need to see that his reports to me correspond to your surveillance. I need to be sure that we can rely on him, that he is thorough, that he is professional."

"Certainly, sir," the agent said quickly. Loki could almost hear his head bobbing up and down enthusiastically in agreement.

"And while you're at it, you might as well dig up all the information that you can on God," Loki added, sounding authoritative.

"Don't disappoint me."

I've grown sloppy of late.

This is dangerous, both to me and to my cause. I must be more careful. I must keep closer watch. His enthusiasm is powerful, and his instincts are keen.

It seems I've vastly underestimated Mr. Montone, which is quite unlike me. Either that or the boy has made one very lucky wild guess. Regardless, he has pieced together the missing information and provided me with a fully assembled puzzle. Without even the benefit of knowing about Gaia's special genetic make up.

It's so obvious, I cannot believe I even needed his assistance. But it's important to have people close to the ground, I think. And while I knew—knew!— that Dr. Rodke was working against my Gaia, stealing from her, looking to profit from her— it did not occur to me that Invince was the missing link.

But of course! His company is a pharmaceutical research company.

He is clearly interested in DNA research and specifically in suppression of fear. Why else would he be interested in my Gaia? Why else would he have convinced her to use her own body as a science experiment, to expose herself to this crippling, debilitating sensation we know as terror?

I've no doubt Rodke's lab facilities are fully equipped with all the latest technology. But no amount of controlled testing can simulate the true human experience. And so—yes!—Rodke is using the scum of the city as his own personal petri dish! He has leaked Invince to the masses. . . *on purpose*. To observe and to chart the results.

Clever. Cunning. Devious. I'm tempted, in fact, to respect his actions but for one thing.

His interest in Gaia cannot be overlooked. It cannot be excused.

Though I am stunned by Jake's abilities, I am also relieved. He has access to Gaia and to her world that I do not. His recon mission will be most helpful—particularly

if he doubts my confidence in him.
He is just on the money, I believe—
but I don't need him to know that.
He'll work harder if he thinks he
still has something to prove. And
thank "God" for that.

Is there some kind of fine line between casual concern and full-on stalking? And if so, how do you know when you've crossed it? Or if you have to ask the question, is it safe to assume that you *have* crossed it, beyond any remaining shadow of doubt?

From the moment I first met Gaia—literally, from the first day I saw her, standing in my high school hallway looking like some fire-breathing dragon (well, okay, an incredibly gorgeous fire-breathing dragon), she's been in some kind of danger. I've seen her chased down by men with guns, and I've seen friends of hers kidnapped and seriously harmed. Hell, not too long ago I *was* one of those friends harmed. I mean, when she says her life is a mess—a *dangerous* mess—she isn't kidding around.

And she's inscrutable. She wants nothing to do with my sympathy. Which, ironically, was what drew me to her in the first place. I understood what it was like to

have to deal with people's BS
false sympathy day in and day out,
from being in a wheelchair. Gaia
didn't treat me the way other people did—and that's the understatement of the year.

But when you're friends with
someone, you want to be there for
them. At least that's the way it
works for me. And I understand not
wanting to talk or to analyze every
last issue. I understand that a lot
of things in her life really suck—I
mean, the girl's lived with at
least three different parental
"figures" in the whole time I've
known her, only one of whom was
actually a parent and *several* of
whom were actively out to get her.

But lately she's been different. Edgy. Insecure. Maybe even a
little depressed. Not the badass
chick I was so impressed by last
fall. And if she doesn't want to talk,
I can't pretend I think it's
okay. I can't pretend I'm not
worried. I can't just let it go
because she isn't ready to deal.
Hence the fine line between gentle

concern and full-on stalking.

You see my dilemma.

I just can't bring myself to believe all of the rumors I've heard about her. I mean, the Village School skanks would spread gossip about Mother Teresa if they were bored enough. There's no reason to put any stock in what Megan and her cronies say. Except. . .

Except that maybe I don't even know Gaia anymore.

There's a part of me that honestly thought, back when we were together, that she still had feelings for Sam. Even though she insisted that she was over him and that they were just friends, seeing the two of them together sparked a crazy, dysfunctional jealousy deep inside. I mean, even to this day I still think they've got an emotional bond. And maybe she can't help it, maybe it's just a part of their connection, but it's there. It came between the two of us when we were together. So who knows? Who knows if she's cheating on Jake? Clearly it's possible to have feelings for more than one person at a time—lots of people do it. I accused her of the very same thing just a short time ago. I mean, sure, she's amazing, and she's my friend, and she's, like, superwoman strong, but at the end of the day she's just a girl. And stuff like this happens to girls and boys sometimes.

Maybe she's not the girl I thought she was.

Or maybe nobody's perfect, and I'm finally starting to see the stitching behind her seams.

No. No way. Who am I kidding? Gaia has lots of characteristics that are less than perfect, but she isn't a liar or a cheater. Say what you will: she's abrasive, she's confrontational, but at the end of the day, if she's anything, she's unpleasantly honest. Brutally straightforward. And I have to give her the benefit of the doubt. Because that's the Gaia I know and love.

How sick is that?

It was an
inexplicable
suspicion—
and it **reduced**
wasn't
levels
going away.
of

testosterone

"CAN YOU PLEASE PASS THE POTATOES?"

Liz asked her mother.

Mrs. Rodke smiled and lifted the silver serving platter, passing the chilled potatoes to her daughter. "I'm so relieved to see you eating carbs. I thought everyone your age avoided them like the devil."

Liz snorted. "Please. Carbohydrates are one of the great joys in my life. I spit in the face of Dr. Atkins—may he rest in peace."

Her mother mock-winced. "That's a lovely image, dear."

"What can I say? I'm a lady," Liz teased. She speared a forkful of potato and chewed away heartily as if to prove her point. She was pretty lucky, she knew, to be able to sit down to dinner with both her parents most nights of the week. She knew plenty of kids her age who communicated with their parents primarily via Post-it notes or whose housekeepers knew their favorite meals by heart. Of course, her mother did have a little help in preparing dinner and running the household, but it was the gesture, the face time, that mattered.

At least, it mattered to Liz. She glanced around the dining-room table, marveling for the umpteenth time at the stunning panoramic view they had of Manhattan. She hoped she never grew tired of that view or began to take it for granted.

Chris and Skyler were clearly less impressed by their parents' attempts at domestic stability. They were both notably absent for dinner.

Even though Skyler was in college and had his own apartment now, he often came home for dinner. And when he wasn't going to make it, he was usually courteous enough to call. The fact that his regular place at the table had been set basically confirmed that he hadn't bothered to do so tonight. *Nice,* Liz thought. She wondered where he was, what he was doing. . . if he was spending another night with Gaia. It was an icky thought, she realized.

It was odd. Chris had been right earlier today, telling Liz she was strangely obsessed. There was no real reason for her to be twitchy about any sort of "thing" between Gaia and Skyler. After all, Gaia was a cool chick, and Skyler. . . well, he was her brother. She loved him. Most of the time.

But for some reason, something about it felt wrong to her. It was an inexplicable suspicion—and it wasn't going away.

Liz swallowed what she was eating before turning to her mother. "Hey, uh—did Chris call to say he wasn't coming home?"

Her mother nodded. "Yes, he was going to a movie and wasn't sure what time it would let out. I set his place just in case. Why—do you want his carbs?"

Liz smiled. "I might."

"What I do wonder," her mother mused, "is what happened to Skyler. It's not like him not to call."

At this, Liz's father turned away from the newspaper he'd been perusing (domestic stability only extended so far—Liz had learned to be tolerant if her father wanted to read at the table). "Oh, nothing to worry about, I'm sure. He probably just met up with some lady friend and lost track of the time."

Liz shuddered. "'Lady friend'? Dad, you are so hip, I can't stand it." *And also, I really hope Gaia isn't the one causing him to lose track of the time. I don't know why I feel that way, but I do. I really, really do.*

"Anyway," her mother continued, refilling her water glass and taking a sip, "I have to confess, I love both of your brothers dearly, but it's nice to have a break from them once in a while. Boys are so loud! It's more peaceful this way, and you and I get to talk more." She smiled wryly. "That is, when you're talking to me and not having a teenage moment."

"Yes, I know how petulant and *adolescent* I can be," Liz said, smiling to show she was teasing. She knew what her mother meant—it *was* peaceful with the reduced levels of testosterone in the air. "But yeah, you're right. Down with boys!" she said, raising a fist in the air.

Her father raised a critical eyebrow in her direction.

"C'mon, Dad," Liz prodded, "I love 'em, but all they ever do is bicker, you know?" Suddenly she found herself turning serious. "I mean, they always have, but don't you think it's gotten worse lately? Is it my imagination or what?"

Dr. Rodke frowned. "I haven't noticed anything."

"Okay, maybe I'm losing my mind, but all of their verbal sparring, all of the little jabs here and there—it just seems a little more acute lately. Like there's some tension going on."

"I can't imagine what it would be," Mrs. Rodke said, sounding worried.

Instantly Liz felt guilty. Being freakishly paranoid was her own cross to bear. It wasn't right to drag her mother into her little mini-drama—especially since it looked like it was all in her mind. "It's probably nothing," she amended. "I'm sure I'm taking one little quarrel and blowing it out of proportion. Forget I said anything."

"Boys will be boys," her mother agreed, waving her hand dismissively.

"It's Darwinian," Dr. Rodke said, his voice carrying the weight of educated authority.

"Ah, the scientist posits a theory," Mrs. Rodke said, winking at her husband.

"Honestly. It's human nature to compete, and the urge is only further exacerbated among brothers. Survival of the fittest, you know."

"Hmmm," Liz said, helping herself to more salad. "If only I'd paid closer attention in biology, I'm sure I'd agree with you."

"I assure you, it's perfectly natural, and it's nothing to worry about," her father insisted. "Chris and Skyler's relationship is just as one would expect between two brothers.

"As your mother says, boys will be boys."

From: gaia13@alloymail.com
To: shred@alloymail.com
Re: All right, all right

You've made your point. If you're just going to go all drama queen on me, then fine, yes, let's hang out. I'll even admit it: I miss you. But you will *not* get me to confess my deep dark secrets. After all, they're secret. I like them that way.

I'll be at school tomorrow, and don't even ask where I've been—I'm serious. But I'm thinking we should hit Benny's Burritos after classes let out. Like a mini-celebration of me actually attending all of my classes. 'Cause you know what? It's damn good to be me.

CHRIS WAS CAREFUL TO TURN HIS

Vaguely Homicidal

key slowly in the lock of the front door as he entered his apartment. It was after eleven, and even if his parents were still awake—which, come to think of it, they probably were—well, it wasn't such a good idea to disturb them. As he passed by the dining room, he could see that a place was still laid out at the table for him and Skyler both. So Skyler hadn't come home for dinner either? Interesting. Chris wondered if there was any truth to Liz's psychotic ramblings at school. What were the chances that Skyler was getting it on with Gaia? Chris had *thought* Gaia had better taste than that—and as Liz pointed out, he had also thought Gaia was dating Jake. Strange days.

Well, Skyler might have Gaia fooled. And he might have their parents fooled—he certainly had their father fooled, at any rate—but Chris wasn't buying it. Anyone who had any expectations of Skyler at all was sure to be disappointed. Skyler Rodke was all form and no substance. Chris saw right through his big brother's sleazy facade. And he was going to bring his brother down.

Chris wandered into the kitchen to see what sort of leftovers from dinner were stashed in the fridge. Apparently the tub of popcorn he had devoured during the movie hadn't done the trick. *Real food,* he thought. *Need real food.* He pulled open the fridge and peeked inside. He saw some squares of something wrapped in tinfoil—baked chicken cutlets, if he had to guess—and some potatoes and salad tucked away in Tupperware containers. Hours past their suggested serving time, they didn't hold too much appeal. *Scratch the real food,* Chris decided. *Do we have any Doritos?*

He closed the door to the refrigerator and jumped.

His father stood in the doorway of the kitchen. And he did not look happy at all.

"Uh, hi," Chris said awkwardly, wondering what the issue was. It couldn't have been that he was out on a school night—please!—and he had even told his parents where he was going. But his father was looking `vaguely homicidal.`

"Sit down," Dr. Rodke hissed, his features dark with anger. "We need to talk."

"Um, okay," Chris said, casting a last, desperate glance toward the snack cabinet. *No Doritos, then. Okay, maybe later.* He lowered himself onto a stool at the island in the center of the room.

"You have problems with Skyler," his father stated baldly. It wasn't a question.

"What?" Chris asked, defensive. "What are you talking about?"

Dr. Rodke sighed. "I'm not going to get into this with you, Chris. The fact is that you have strong,

.

strong issues with your brother. You're jealous. You feel a need to compete."

"I don't. . . ," Chris began, before a flash of anger overtook him. "I mean, even if I do—what do you care? Can you blame me? You make it pretty clear that he's your favorite. He's the one you're grooming to take over the company. Since when do you give a *crap* about my 'issues' with Skyler?" he demanded. "Since when can you even be bothered to notice me?"

Instantly his father was in Chris's face, looming. "I noticed, dear son, when it stopped being subtle. I noticed when your sister and your mother noticed. Believe me, I tried to ignore it. I tried to tell myself that it was simple sibling rivalry and that it would fade. But I'm not so sure anymore. And frankly, I'm not interested."

Chris opened his mouth to speak, then closed it. He was dumbfounded. And pissed.

"You want therapy, Chris? We'll get you therapy. I can get you the best shrink in the city, the best that money can buy. But whatever you need to do to get over this, you *will* get over it.

"Because I won't stand for it."

"But—," Chris tried to interject.

Dr. Rodke wasn't listening. "What you don't seem to realize, my boy, is that your problems, your petty grievances. . . well, they've begun to affect me. And that's unacceptable. I don't know if you're aware, but running an international pharmaceutical company can be something of a high-profile affair. Lots of mentions in the media, lots of people looking out.

"I have to be sure that when they look, they see nothing but a sterling image reflected back at them. And that includes my family. That includes you."

Chris folded his arms and regarded his father sullenly, silent.

"I won't pretend that I'm especially interested in why you're suddenly feeling so competitive. I don't care. It's in your mind, and I'm far too busy to be bothered. But the point is—and listen to me well, Chris—the point is this: it ends now. I don't want to hear your sister talking about how 'weird' things are between you and your brother. I don't want *anyone* to notice anything of the sort. To the casual observer— even to the practiced interloper—we are the perfect, happy family. No matter what."

"So you snap your fingers and just like that all of my feelings go away?" Chris retorted.

"Oh, yes," Dr. Rodke assured him. "They most certainly will. Because trust me when I say that whatever's got you so bent out of shape? Well, Chris, I can make it much, much worse."

He patted Chris on the head, then reached above him to the cabinet over his head and pulled out a bag of Cool Ranch Doritos. He extended his arm, offering the bag to Chris. Chris took it, though his appetite was essentially ruined. "Whatever," Chris said.

Dr. Rodke shot Chris a look that instantly made him rethink his attitude. "Just trust me on this, Chris. I can't have any bad press, and I *won't* take any attitude. So get it together. Or else."

Okay, so here's a question—
which flavor of Doritos do you
prefer? Nacho Cheese or Cool
Ranch? Don't over-think it; just
the first response that comes to
your mind.

Dumb question? Not so much,
actually. And don't try to tell me
that you like them both. Because
in the split second after I posed
the query, there was a moment when
a very particularly flavored corn
chip danced before your eyes.
Maybe it came in a red bag. Or
maybe it came in a blue one. But
it was one and not the other. For
at least a split second.

Because that's the way it
goes. That's the nature of the
beast. When someone says to you,
"Oh, whichever, I don't mind,"
chances are that on some level,
they're flat-out lying. Okay,
sure, maybe the truth of the matter is that ultimately they'd be
happy to eat sushi instead of
Chinese or vice versa. Maybe it's
not a life-or-death decision. But

they *do* have a proclivity, however slight. There was a momentary flash of, "Gee, an egg roll
might be nice," before they realized that some crab tempura could
do the trick just the same.

That's the thing about choices:
they force a person to choose.

When you're given more than
one option, one of the two will
seem more appealing. Maybe it's
not a value thing, maybe it's not
really a judgment, but you're
going to lean in one direction or
the other. At least for a moment.

And that's the way it is with
brothers.

Specifically, that's the way
it is with Skyler and me. In some
way, our father has chosen one of
us over the other.

I wish it weren't that way. I
truly wish we were one big, happy
family the way that everyone
thinks. Liz is funny and my friend
as well as my sister, and my mom—
well, I'm one of the kids that
means it when I say my mom is
great. For real. But Skyler. Ugh.

I don't know if I'd hate him so much if it weren't for my father. "There's room for us all in the company," Liz says, parroting the party line. Yeah, sure. There's room for all of us to sit on a board nodding like a bunch of bob-bleheads and deciding which phil-anthropies are going to reap the benefits of our big, honking checking account. There's room for us all to make a salary and sit pretty for the rest of our natural lives. And I'm not knocking that.

But Skyler's going to be numero uno, and I just don't think I can stand it.

I don't know why Liz is okay with things the way they are. Maybe it's because she's youngest, and she's a girl. Maybe in some twisted way she feels that Skyler is entitled to this? Entitled? For being born first? Hell, no.

Skyler and I, we're brothers. We get compared. Skyler's "the older one" (not his fault, really—even I can admit that), and I'm "the witty one." He's

"the good-looking one" and I'm
"the cute one." All perfectly
respectable compliments. But come
on, admit it: you've got us
ranked in your mind. You're keeping tabs, keeping track.

I'm okay with being "cute" and
"witty." What I'm not okay with
is being an "also-ran."
Unfortunately, it's just a function of being a brother. A
younger brother.

But there are plenty of other
adjectives that could be used to
describe me. And soon my father
and Skyler will know who I really
am. As in, "the smart one," "the
cunning one," "the devious one."

"The one who surprised them all."

"Boys will be boys," my wife says, and she's right. I never set out to create a competitive paradigm for my two sons. From the moment they were born, I loved them both equally and wanted them both to thrive.

Certainly not at my own expense, however. And it seems that's what at stake—my own reputation, my company, my empire—even, perhaps, my legacy.

I know it's been hard for Chris. He isn't the firstborn son, he isn't the youngest, the coddled little girl that Liz is. Classic middle-child syndrome, and I was sensitive to his needs. But I have my breaking point.

There was room for Chris in my plans, in the future of Rodke and Simon. I know my son feels that he's being edged out since Skyler is poised to take over the mantle once I step down. What can I say? It's true—I plan for Skyler to be my VP, my second in command. He has a knack for it, and I believe

in playing to people's skills;
it's part of how I built the company into the phenomenal success
that it is. But Chris had his own
role; he was going to be involved.
I pegged him as a distributor—and
might I say, my instincts were
quickly proven to be valid. Chris
was good at his job. Almost too
good. And now he's getting greedy.

I'm not a monster. I'm not
heartless or cruel. I have no
interest in seeing my own son suffer from delusions of inadequacy.
But neither will I stand by as his
own sloppiness, his own jealousy
and insecurity threaten to expose
my work before its time. Hopefully
he heard me when I spoke. Hopefully
he processed my warning. Because I
won't repeat myself. And I won't
stand for any more of this. Rodke
and Simon needs to be a seamless
operation. No unwanted attention
from the outside over interfamily
strife will be tolerated.

If "God" doesn't have himself a
reality check and fast, well. . .
there will be hell to pay.

This wasn't all that terribly out of the ordinary for Washington Square Park.

are you kidding

Top Five Reasons People Have Hunted Me Down

1. Jealousy/resentment. (Ella, Tatiana—both were pissed that someone was more interested in me than in them.)
2. Payback. (Skizz, the skin- heads in the park—Skizz was pissed that I took Mary away from him as a drug buyer; the skinheads were pissed that I was always breaking up their tea parties in Washington Square.)*
3. Personal advancement. (George Niven—not quite sure, though, what he was going to get out of the deal.)
4. Pure, unadulterated mental instability. (Loki—first had some strange competition thing with my father, then saw me as my mother's legacy—never mind that he killed her to begin with—then wanted to harness my strange bio- chemistry for his own evil pur- poses. Yuck.)
5. ???**

    *It is important to note the number of people I seem to piss off on a daily basis.
    **Will have to come back to this one. Skyler's meeting is tomorrow. TBD then.

    I'm sure I'm missing something.
    Oh, well. The list will still be here when I remember. There's always room for more.

ED WAS STARTING TO FEEL A LITTLE

bit awkward about the amount of time he was spending star- ing at Gaia's locker. Wasn't it only yesterday that he had been in this very same posi- tion, concentrating fiercely on the space in front of her locker as if he could will her to materialize?

More Than Borderline Sad

Today was different, though. Today he and Gaia actually had plans. They had e-mailed. She had been willing to meet him. Yet here he was, concentrating fiercely on the space in front of her locker, feeling like some kind of chump, a massive glutton for punishment. Was there something wrong with him? he wondered. Did he have some sort of freakish disease? One that drove him toward unassuming young women who had demonstrated little interest in being his friend? Because this was starting to become more than borderline sad. Friendships implied, by basic definition, a certain level of mutual interest.

"Gaia late?" Ed heard a voice from behind him ask in a saccharine-sweet voice. "Or did she not even bother showing up for school again?"

Ed turned to see Megan standing behind him, looking like a refugee from *The O.C.* in a skirt so short, it might better be called a belt, and a bright, strappy tank top that presumed a warmer climate than Manhattan's in May. Was she hoping to be spotted by the next reality-television guru and squired off to a farm in Iowa to play Paris or Nicole? Ed shuddered. "Why, were you looking for her?" he asked in a much less sarcastic tone than he would have liked, knowing full well that she hadn't been.

Megan raised a contemptuous eyebrow. "Duh, of course not."

"Really feelin' the love, Megan," Ed heard. The wooden tone tinged with apathy could only belong to one person. He turned again to see that indeed, Gaia had crept up behind them while they were exchanging "pleasantries." Her timing was impeccable. But even if it hadn't been, she wouldn't have seemed any less the goddess, emerging as she did with her ratty ponytail `still managing to bounce like in an "after" shot in a shampoo commercial.` Ed grinned at her.

"Wasn't sure where you were," he acknowledged. Not that it mattered. The sad truth was that all Ed cared about was that Gaia was here now. "Burritos?"

Gaia gave him an `are-you-kidding` smile. "I'm *starving*," she said, acquiescing. God, he adored her overwhelmingly indelicate appetite.

"Benny's it is," Ed said. He offered his bent elbow to her. She reached out and chucked him lightly on the bicep, then slid her own arm into the crook of his. For a moment he imagined that they were going to skip to Benny's. After all, it took a lot to embarrass Gaia.

Or at least, once upon a time it had.

"*Ugh*," Megan groaned, sounding world weary. "What is with you, Gaia? Does Jake even mind that you're off on a date with your latest boyfriend du jour?"

Ed cringed but couldn't stop himself from glancing over to see how Gaia had taken the blow. Annoyance flashed across her exotic features, but only for an instant. She straightened and squared her shoulders. "Salsa fresca," she said decisively to Ed. She pulled him toward the side doors without another nod in Megan's direction. "I want extra salsa fresca."

"THAT'S A LOT OF SALSA FRESCA,"

Ed noted as Gaia popped the lid off a plastic container, infusing their immediate surroundings with the clean scent of cilantro and ripe tomatoes.

Boyfriend du Jour

"Yes, well, I did ask for 'extra,'" Gaia reminded Ed mock-sarcastically. She unwrapped her burrito, laying the wax paper carefully down on the grass between the two of them for a casual picnic in Washington Square. Ed briefly reflected on how, not too long ago, this sort of after-school snack attack thing had been par for the course for the two of them.

Gaia fished a greased-stained brown paper bag from inside the larger plastic takeout bag. "Look at all the oil," she exclaimed gleefully, shaking open the bag and releasing a few freshly fried tortilla chips onto the paper next to her burrito. She scooped up a handful and crunched away enthusiastically. "Perfection," she pronounced, nodding in grave endorsement. "Two thumbs up."

Ed reached over and snatched a few away from her. "Me too." He munched in contentment.

Gaia swallowed and made a face, as if suddenly remembering something. "So, what the hell was Megan going on about before? I mean, I try not to put too much stock in anything she says, but what the hell? Boyfriend du jour?"

Ed thought for a minute before replying. But hadn't that been the whole point in inviting Gaia out to begin with? He might as well be straight with her. If they didn't have honesty, then really—what did they have in their friendship after all? "Um, I don't know exactly what she meant," he began carefully. "But maybe—and this is just a guess, you know—maybe it has something to do with how much time you spend with Skyler Rodke these days."

Gaia instantly flushed, color flooding her cheeks.

"Oh," she mumbled. "Yeah, I guess I have been hanging around with him a lot lately."

Ed peered at her with curiosity. Her stormy eyes were a deep gray rather than their usual green-blue hybrid. Gray couldn't be a great sign, he decided. "Well, look, G," he said with a sigh. "I don't think you really need to waste any time worrying about what Megan and her friends say about you—or anyone else for that matter. But people *are* talking. And not just the FOHs, you know. And sure, I don't care about gossip, and I think you *definitely* don't care about gossip. But with so many people saying the same thing, I have to wonder if there isn't the tiniest grain of truth to the rumors. I mean, are you interested in Skyler? Are you involved with him? What does Jake think? Do you even *care* what Jake thinks?"

Ed took a deep breath as clouds formed across Gaia's features. He was taking a huge gamble, he knew, by asking her such personal questions. Gaia hated personal questions. But if there was anything going on, he wanted her to know she could talk to him.

"Gaia, I know I might be crossing the line even asking these questions. You can totally tell me to take a hike if you want. I just think. . . well, I just want you to be happy," he finished finally. His words, suspended in the space between the two of them, seemed woefully insufficient now that he'd voiced them aloud. He wondered if he had taken the right approach.

"Ed," Gaia started slowly, "that hike you were talking about? Please take it." Ed could tell she was teasing. But that didn't mean she was willing to bare her soul. She gave a weak and unconvincing half smile. "Get gone." She toyed with the edge of her frayed T-shirt and looked away. She sighed heavily. It seemed to Ed that she was wavering, contemplating taking down some of the walls she'd built around herself.

Gaia coughed and made a small throat-clearing sound, jutting her chin out a bit defiantly.

"*God is dead!*"

The voice was little more than a throaty whisper, but as it sounded, Gaia and Ed found themselves confronted by a knee thundering squarely into their chips and salsa fresca. Suddenly a small, grungy-looking girl was face-to-face with Gaia, and she didn't look e s p e - c i a l l y w e l l - b a l a n c e d. "Dead, dead, dead," she repeated tonelessly, almost chanting.

The girl, whoever she was, reached out and grabbed Gaia's collar, steadying herself with her opposite arm on the grass. "Do you know him?" She giggled.

Gaia blinked in disbelief. "Do I know *God*?" she asked incredulously. "Not so much." She shrugged.

Ed could see Gaia didn't think this girl was really a threat. But still, how had she landed between them so suddenly? How had they managed not to see her coming? Wasn't Gaia supposed to be, like, trained to sense her enemies? Clearly Gaia didn't think of this girl as much of an enemy. Or maybe she'd been too distracted by his *Law & Order*–style interrogation, he thought guiltily. At least this situation looked pretty manageable.

A small *click* sounded, and Ed looked up to see that God Girl now held a small switchblade to Gaia's side. *Okay, less manageable,* he thought, panicking.

"*I need him,*" the girl shrieked. No one in the park seemed to even register that anything out of the ordinary was going on. Of course, this wasn't all that terribly out of the ordinary for Washington Square Park.

Damn, damn, damn, Ed thought. He didn't want to make any sudden moves and propel this girl—or her nice shiny knife—straight into Gaia. What were his other choices? He'd only been out of the wheelchair for a few months now, and it wasn't like he had been the Terminator before his injury. *Damn.*

Gaia didn't look frightened, however. Just pissed. "Trust me, you don't want to get into this," she said coolly.

"You can't hurt me," the girl whispered. "Even if God's not here. I have his secret medicine." She drew back her arm, preparing to stab Gaia. "NOW TELL ME WHERE HE IS," she bellowed.

Gaia reached out reflexively and grabbed the girl's wrist, immobilizing the blade mere inches from her waist. She twisted and the fingers splayed, dropping the knife to the ground. Ed leaned forward and snatched it up snapping the blade safely back into the handle and clutching it for dear life.

In one smooth move Gaia pulled the girl's other hand off her collar, raised herself to her feet, and yanked the girl up with her.

"My knife!" the girl cried, as if just realizing that it had been taken from her.

"It's his knife now," Gaia informed her, nodding toward Ed. "Finders keepers, losers weepers." She let go of the girl's wrist and whaled on her, `slamming her fist into God Girl's stomach.`

"Oof," the girl moaned, stumbling backward. She glared at Gaia, her eyes narrowed to slits. "What the hell was *that*?" She charged forward, furious.

Gaia stretched out one leg and stomped on the girl's foot, sending her forward with the force of her own momentum. The girl did a heavy face-plant into the grass, and Gaia kicked at her. Ed noted that Gaia still seemed more irritated than anything else.

Gaia stormed forward and stood over the girl menacingly. "Seriously," she said.

"Get gone."

Oookay.

It looks like Gaia's back.

I still have not the foggiest idea what the *hell* was going on with her the last few weeks, but something tells me that's not going to be cleared up for me anytime soon. Which, I suppose, is okay, because old Gaia is the one that I know and love, and hey—perfect timing! Thrilled to have ya back, sister!

No joke.

The park hasn't been the safest place for me and for those near and dear, but for as many times as something shady has gone down for me, there have been an equal number of times that Gaia has come swooping in like Wonder Woman (though, sadly, without the gold bustier) and saved the day.

Gaia Moore is, like, my hero.

And she's back! How can I complain? She's surly, she's unreliable, she sticks to no one's schedule but her own. She dresses, uh, for comfort, totally

unaware of her own gorgeosity,
and she's got the social graces
of a leper. She can't be bothered
with other people's opinions of
her, and she doesn't take BS. And
if you mess with her or (dare I
flatter myself) her friends—
she'll kick your ass.

Hallelujah!

Well, in that case, Fargo, I
ask myself, *what could possibly
be your damage?*

My damage? It's simple. *Self,*
I say (on those rare occasions
when I'm inclined to talk to
myself, I'm equally inclined to
answer. I mean, it's only polite,
right?), *why the hell can't you
ever get through to Gaia?*

I'm selfish, I suppose.
Narcissistic. Clearly Gaia is better
off as Miss Independent. Clearly she
is just fine without needing to hug
and share and talk and grow. So my
desperate need to be her sole confi-
dant, her savior (as if!), is completely egocentrically motivated.

Human nature is a bitch, right?
But I'd like to think I have

something to offer her as a
friend. I'd like to think that if
she could bring herself to open up
to me, I could find a way to give
to her. It would mean something.
She would benefit and take comfort. Not to stray too far into
delusions of sainthood, but. . .
yeah, it'd be nice to give something back. And since the idea of
me busting out like Indiana Jones
and saving *her* in the next knife
fight is looking reasonably
unlikely, this may be all I have.

Why doesn't she want it?

Or maybe she does. A part of me
still believes that she does. I
mean, she *must*. It's against the
laws of God and man not to want to
take comfort in one's friends,
right? *Right?* It's sociological, or
anthropological, or. . . or. . .
pathological. Some sort of "-logi-
cal," for sure. I mean, it makes
sense. Humans need other humans.
Adam needed Eve. Frankenstein
needed the Bride. Nick needs
Jessica.

Okay, maybe scratch that last

one. But you see where I'm going
with this.

True, the couples I've named
above are:

1. romantically involved
rather than platonic; and

2. fictitious (with the exception
of Nick and Jessica, who are just,
well. . . really, really scary).

But I'm onto something. I'm
sure of it. And the look in
Gaia's eyes just before Jesus
Freak came flying out of the
clear blue sky and sailing into
our salsa fresca ("extra,
please") told me she was getting
ready to open up. To unload.

And now we've missed our
moment.

Maybe I'm expecting too much.
Maybe it's unreasonable for me to
think that a friendship is always
completely egalitarian.
(*Egalitarian*. Good use of SAT
word, Fargo. And you were afraid
that Kaplan class wouldn't come
in handy once the hellish tests
were over.) Obviously whatever
the typical "rules" of friendship

are, they don't apply to Gaia.
Obviously I'm going to have to
allow her some flexibility if I
want her in my life. I thought I
was starting to understand her,
to get what makes her tick, but
who was I kidding? I've barely
scratched the surface. I'm still
way back in Gaia 101. I've got to
understand her before we can move
forward.

I've got to learn her rules.

I've got to learn her rules
before we can break them.

From: megan21@alloymail.com
To: tammiejammie@alloymail.com
Re: Guess

Who I ran into on my way out of school today.
Fargo looking pathetic, as usual, waiting by
Gaia's locker. Doesn't he know how cute he is? He
can do soooo much better than that freak! Anyway,
he was just sulking around, I guess, when who
should saunter in but Queen G herself? Suppose
she decided to grace him with her presence. I
mean, aren't they supposed to be best friends?

Or are they even friends? Like you can even be
friends with someone after you break up with
them. Like he's not still totally in love with
her. And she can't even be bothered to settle on
one guy. She has to juggle three people she's not
even good enough for. Will wonders never cease? I
mean, how *does* she do it?

Not that I care, anyway.

From: tammiejammie@alloymail.com
To: megan21@alloymail.com
Re: Totally

We are totally not caring, girl! Okay, yes, Gaia's game really gets under my skin—I mean, she is completely undeserving of the male attention that she gets, *especially* what with how she plays everyone—but we can't waste our time thinking about it. We've got *prom* coming up, and graduation! And now college to look forward to. And college boys. Or should I say, college *men*? Really, how much more insignificant will Gaia Moore be to us in the grand scheme of things once we're outta here?

She is nothing. Once a loser, always a loser. We have way bigger fish to fry.

From: tammiejammie@alloymail.com
To: jakem@alloymail.com
Re: Manly man things

Jake—

I *hate* to bother you, but as you may know, I'm
on the prom committee, and, well, I've got a
manly man task that needs taking care of. Josh
Mayer lent me some speakers—I know the DJ has his
own, but these are supposedly *killer*—and we need
to transport them to the hotel. I mean, I should
be able to just shove them in a cab, but the
thing is, I can't really lift them. I know, so
lame, but what can I say? I mean, I think the
speakers weigh more than I do.

I'm appealing to your sense of chivalry, dude.
What do you say?

ps: Megan told me that she saw Gaia go off with
Ed this afternoon after school. I think it's
great that she's out and about again—I know she's
not always. . . *consistent* with attendance. I'm
sure you were glad to see her in the hallways
since you're always so inseparable.

From: jakem@alloymail.com
To: tammiejammie@alloymail.com
Re: Favor

    Yeah, okay. I've got some things to take care
of in the next few days, but if it can wait until
the weekend, sure.

Something
about this
God guy
left a bad
taste in
his mouth.

**urban
decay**

JAKE SQUINTED INTO THE DAWNING

sunlight once more before glancing again first at the digital wristwatch he was sporting and then back to the clock on the BlackBerry Oliver had loaned to him. Yep, three seconds had passed since the last time he checked his watch. It was officially 6:02:03. God was late.

Lifestyles of Urban Drug Pushers

He was being crazy, he knew. It wasn't like any of his watches, though synchronized, were set to, like, the universal clock or whatever (which, come to think of it, might just be an urban myth, anyway—he'd have to look into that). And though his knowledge of the lifestyles of urban drug pushers was blessedly limited, he wasn't totally sure whether or not punctuality was high on their list of priorities. Sighing impatiently and stealing another glance at his watch, he guessed not. Oliver would have *never* stood for this kind of laziness.

Jake was feeling testier than usual, even for a mission like this. He couldn't put his finger on it, but something about this God guy left a bad taste in his mouth. A very bad taste. It didn't help that the sky was a clear, cloudless blue, birds were chirping, and the park was actually, for once, populated with lolling, peaceful people who weren't involved in anything unsavory—just people out to enjoy a pleasant New York morning. *What are the odds?* Jake mused, savoring the irony.

Generally a bright, sunny day in the city would have been a welcome anomaly. Summertime in Manhattan generally brought with it steamy humidity that somehow coaxed the headier smells of urban decay to the forefront. Stale urine, garbage, body odor. . . these were Jake's fun-time-in-the-summer associations. So these springlike conditions should have been a sheer joy. But instead they were feeding into his anxiety. So incongruous was the sunshine with the task at hand that Jake found the whole experience just that damn much more disconcerting.

6:03:57.

Not only did Jake not see anyone he suspected was God, but he also didn't see anyone who looked like he or she might be waiting to meet with God, which seemed pretty strange, too. True, he had heard that God only dealt with top-level dealers. But why weren't any of them skulking in the shadows, waiting for him to make his grand appearance? Or *were* they? Could Jake possibly have gotten *that* sloppy? From behind him a tree branch snapped under the weight of someone's foot, and he whirled around.

It was a dog. A freakin' yellow Lab.

Okay, so not God, Jake thought, breathing deeply. *Not even close.*

He wasn't sure how long to give this man to appear. After all, there was no law saying that God had to be on time. Chances were that he made his own rules and held to his own schedule and that everyone else just worked around him. He could cruise by at seven and not have to worry about jeopardizing his client base.

Or. . . he could not show up at all. After all, what was Jake even basing his suspicions on? The ramblings of a lunatic, that's what. Real reliable sources. So how long, then, until he gave up?

Gave up, admitted defeat. . . and crawled back to Oliver in supplication.

Yeah, right, Jake thought. He'd turn to stone waiting here for some sign of God if that was what it should come to rather than admit to Oliver that he'd fallen short. That he hadn't been able to hack it.

Jake sighed again. At least there was always cool people-watching to be done in the park. For instance, that yellow Lab was really kinda cute, gnawing away on the branch he'd ripped up before. And his owner—a lithe redhead anticipating the season in a strappy tank top—wasn't too bad, either.

And what about. . . Jake stiffened. It had been a gamble, standing where he was, to the north of the fountain. Who was to say that this was for sure where God was going to be? Jake had decided to come to this part of the park because this was where his strung-out little informant had stood the other day. And look at that—he seemed to be having a bit of luck.

Jake could hardly have missed the man who was slowly but surely moving into the frame. After all, he wore a long, black trench coat and dark glasses. *Very cliché,* Jake couldn't help but think. His hair was a bright, spiky shade of blue. And now he was leaning casually against a tree and lighting a cigarette.

Blue hair and a weird, long jacket weren't so incredibly novel, so hugely bizarre, against the backdrop of Washington Square Park. Just in front of the fountain Jake could see a man break dancing to the Sex Pistols (no small feat), dressed entirely in gold lamé. Blue hair wasn't exactly extreme. But it was the *way* that the man tilted himself so lightly against the tree. As if he didn't have a concern in the world. As if he were the cat that had eaten the canary.

As if he were waiting for someone.

Jake inhaled sharply. He wasn't a top agent. The things he'd learned from Oliver at this point would probably fill no more than a matchbook. But he had instincts. And his instincts were telling him that Blue Hair was God.

Jake hunched down on his heels, trying to seem small. He didn't want God to notice him, but he didn't want to lose his vantage point. He readied himself.

It was game time.

OH GOD.

It was so annoying. People were *so annoying*. Junkies were most annoying of all.

Most Annoying of All

God had only a handful of people to meet today, and as usual, he'd staggered his business hours. He didn't like the idea of people waiting for him in one massively long line of freak show druggies—each more stark raving than the next, the entire pathetic crew of them practically foaming at the mouth. No good, not exactly subtle. So he gave them each very distinct times—very *carefully* plotted-out times. It was all very deliberate. After all, he certainly couldn't be seen chilling out all morning—that would attract altogether too much of the wrong kind of attention.

So where the hell was Zan, then? He'd arranged to meet her at six, and it was now six-fifteen. *She* was probably the most annoying of them all—a party girl past her prime who didn't even realize that the party was over, the booze had dried up, and the record on the turntable was skipping. She wasn't even a dealer any more. But he was willing to keep her on as a client because she purchased in volume. He ran his fingers through his hair, exasperated. She had exactly four minutes to get to the park. He didn't *need* her business, after all. He didn't *really* need anyone's business, for that matter. He didn't need the money—he just needed half the city hooked on Invince. That was his job, and in that sense he was practically a workaholic.

He looked up. *There* she was. *Stupid cow,* he thought. She was loping across the grass unevenly—like a vampire, she responded to daylight like she would to an allergen, one arm flung upward to ward off any potential vitamin D. Her bleached-blond hair bounced stiffly against her shoulders. Her stark makeup caked at the corners of her mouth and eyes, making her look like a caricature of herself. God, he hated her. She looked nervous. *Good.*

But. . . something was off. Something in the air. Someone was watching him, he could tell. God had spent enough years in the public eye to know what it felt like to be the subject of someone's gaze. But who? Who could possibly care? Some lame-ass ex-con on halfway-house community service, picking bits of plastic foam litter off the grass and jonesing for a dime bag of weed? As if God could be bothered with such trivialities.

No. God's eyes narrowed. *There.* Crouched against a tree, thinking he looked so suave and smooth. Thinking he blended. Wearing a white shirt. Against a tree. God knew that face.

God sat next to that face twice a day, come to think of it.

God could easily put a name to that face.

Jake Montone.

Jake Montone had seen him. And if the expression on his face was any indication, Jake knew exactly who God was.

AS A GENERAL RULE, ZAN WASN'T

an especially observant person. Drugs, alcohol, and other mainstays of her hard-partying lifestyle had dulled her senses starting way back in junior high. It was ironic, actually. Drugs were what had killed any remnant of genuine emotion within her, but at the same time, drugs were what she now used to dredge up artificial sensations. She was wholly self-managed and wholly self-medicated to adapt to her surroundings as she saw fit. *Wouldn't have it any other way,* she thought as she crossed the thick patches of grass that constituted one of the many "lawns" of Washington Square Park. She rubbed her elbows with her palms absently.

At present, her primary concern was that she was late to meet God, which even she, within the deep recesses of her sluggish consciousness, was aware was

Not Good. Tardiness was definitely frowned upon by God. And however ridiculous, however wannabe badass tough she knew God was, she wanted to stay on his good side. No question about it.

So she wasn't really thinking about her surroundings as she scurried to meet her dealer. If anything, the sunlight felt too bright against her face. As soon as she scored, she planned to retreat back into the dark, cozy cavern of her bedroom at the boardinghouse. But she happened to glance up at a particular moment, hoping to get a sense of exactly how impatient God was growing. Scale of one to ten and all. And that was when she saw it.

It all happened in the blink of an eye. Thankfully, Zan's eyes were at that exact moment widened, peering, the pupils dilated, though barely comprehending. But she sharpened up fast. Because she saw God. He was leaning against a tree, in his typical hipper-than-thou posture.

And he looked decidedly cross.

She followed his gaze, and her heart caught in her chest.

There, not ten feet away, was Gaia's hunky boyfriend, Jake. Gaia's *stupid* hunky boyfriend. Who did he think he was? Did he think God couldn't see him, out in plain sight, stalking? Please. Okay, so maybe he wasn't dressed like Big Bird (which, even in

Washington Square Park, might have stood out a little), but he wasn't, like, *invisible*.

And he certainly wasn't invisible to God.

Zan looked at God and saw him see Jake. And she looked at Jake and saw Jake see God. To her mind the scene unfolded as if in slow motion. God blinked, then straightened, casual and aloof. Jake shook his head slightly, then backed away. The two studiously avoiding looking at each other again. They were pretending now that they hadn't seen each other. But they had. And Zan—Zan, who hardly ever knew anything other than where and what to score and maybe where to go to party—Zan knew it.

Oh jeez. Oh my God. No pun intended, but oh. . . my. . . *God*.

That girl, that girl was wrong: God's not dead.

God is *Chris*.

Chris Rodke is God. Chris Rodke is dealing drugs. Chris Rodke is dealing *Invince*.

But why?

This discovery basically confirms a few key points:

1. The Rodkes are definitely behind Invince.

2. The Rodkes are definitely after Gaia.

3. There must be some connection between Gaia and their Invince research.

But what?

It's like I've just opened a five-hundred-piece puzzle and turned it over onto my bed. All of the pieces are *right there*, and they all fit together to make a bigger picture. A picture that will be revealed to me clear as day just as soon as all the pieces fall into place.

Which they will. They *have to*.
They're made to fit together.
They're *supposed* to fit together.
I just have to figure out how.
And I have to figure out how
before God comes after me.

Memo

From: C
To: L
Re: Problem

The boy was tracked maintaining surveillance of one "God" in Washington Square Park from 0:6:00 hours until 0:6:45. However, his undercover work was not undercover enough. J was spotted by his mark, and all evidence suggests he was recognized. This could be a problem. First, the boy may be in physical danger, depending on God's interest in covering his own tracks. Further, he may have exposed our work.

Please advise ASAP.

Memo

From: L
To: C
Re: Problem

Indeed, this is problematic. Need confirmation
that J was in fact recognized, and need to ascer-
tain the lengths to which God will go in order to
maintain anonymity. Please monitor and report
back.

From: jakem@alloymail.com
To: gaia13@alloymail.com
Re: Your new friends

Gaia—

I don't want to say too much over e-mail, and I
don't want to worry you or get you all panicked,
but I think we need to talk. I know you think I've
been stalking you lately, following you around and
hanging out at the boardinghouse talking to your
housemates. I know you think I've crossed some
lines, and when I apologized, Gaia, I meant it.
But we need to talk, and soon.

I'm sure all of the trash I've talked about
Skyler seems like petty jealousy. I don't blame you
for being dismissive or pissed. But I think I'm on
to something, and whether you like it or not, I've
got some news. News I think you should hear.

Believe it or not, Gaia, I don't exactly *enjoy*
being right (well, not in this case). But unfortunately, I'm pretty sure I am. I'm pretty sure
you're in danger. Can we meet? Can we talk?

I'm going to come by the boardinghouse
tonight. Please, please be there.

Gaia, I'm worried.

—J

Jake Montone is not a stupid guy. Granted, I don't know the boy all that well, and maybe I haven't been totally, one hundred percent sober each and every encounter we've had. And to be perfectly honest, most of the encounters that I've had with him have involved him demanding to know where Gaia is and me refus-ing to tell him. (Just for kicks. Evil, I know.) But from what I've seen, Jake isn't dumb.

I don't think he meant for God to see him. He couldn't have. I think, then, that he must have been taken by surprise. Whoever he knows God to be—whatever external context they have for each other—it just blew Jake away. So much so that he couldn't help but stare and stare.

And now he's done.

I don't mean to be dramatic, and normally I wouldn't think twice about God. God is clearly a low-level dealer who stumbled on the stash of the century—who had any idea that Invince would be the phenomenon it's become? Who knows how the hell God has such unlimited—and exclusive—access to the stuff? But he's no career criminal. He's no street thug. Ordinarily I wouldn't even give it a second thought.

Except I know a thing or two about dealers. And however unaccustomed God is to exacting a little ultraviolence, something tells me that now that his identity has been compromised, he may just be willing to make an exception. To learn.

To learn to kick Jake's ass.

And Jake, meanwhile, doesn't even know what's coming, what's around the corner. For chrissake, Jake didn't even think to disguise himself this morning!

He's out of his league. And he's about to meet his maker.

Memo

From: J
To: Agent O
Re: God

    Well, I did what you asked—I did some digging
to figure out what I could about God. And did I
ever get the dirt!

    It's just like we figured—the Rodkes are
behind *all* of this! I tracked the Invince dealer
that everyone buys from—he has some sort of
exclusive handle on the drug. I followed him to
the park. And who should it be? None other than
Chris Rodke!

    I still have no idea what the point is in
leaking Invince onto the street. I have no idea
what Invince is really intended for. I have no
idea why Skyler has been manipulating Gaia and
what she has to do with Invince. But it's safe to
say that the Rodkes are in deep.

    What do you think?

Memo

From: Agent O
To: J
Re: God

What do I think? What I think, dear boy, is that we have our work cut out for us.

You said it yourself—we still don't know what Invince is intended for or why it's being leaked on the streets. We don't know how Gaia fits into this picture. This new information is only one piece of the puzzle. But it's certainly a start.

Of course, if you were able to identify Chris Rodke, one has to ask whether or not Chris was able to identify you? This could be dangerous. Please keep me apprised.

Well, I'll be damned.

The boy actually did it.

Not to say that I didn't expect him to—I wouldn't have wasted his time or mine if I didn't think there was anything for him to learn. (Actually, that's not *quite* true. I would never have wasted my own time, to be sure, but I suppose there's no guarantee that I wouldn't have wasted his.) True, I was skeptical of his theory that the Rodkes were connected to God. But I didn't necessarily think we'd get this lucky. I didn't think the boy had it in him.

Rodke and Simon Pharmaceuticals is interested in manipulating my Gaia's DNA.

Skyler Rodke has ingratiated himself with Gaia, insinuating himself into her daily doings to the exclusion of other friends and activities (which were, admittedly, few, but no matter. . .).

And someone in that household is after her DNA.

DELIVER

One assumes that Dr. Rodke has told Chris to "leak" the drug onto the street deliberately. Human reaction is certainly a more accurate gauge than any insights a lab rat could afford. One assumes that Skyler is keeping Gaia close so as to harvest samples of her DNA. The same could be said for Liz. One assumes.

But I've learned never to rely too heavily on assumptions.

We are closer than ever, and all because of the boy. I'll admit, whatever rein I gave him, I didn't ever truly allow myself to imagine these results. I was foolish and shortsighted.

I won't make the same mistake twice.

The picture is still muddy; there's work to be done yet. I'll need Jake's assistance, but I'll need to watch my step. The more he knows, the more of a liability he is. It's a delicate balance.

Fortunately, I'm nothing if not an acrobat.

A gleaming, sooty eye pressed against the door, regarding Jake with scrutiny.

voice of reason

JAKE WAS FEELING UNCERTAIN

Unconvincing Facsimile

as he rapped on the door of the boardinghouse on Bank Street. He hadn't heard back from Gaia since he'd sent his semi-frantic missive. That made the chances of her actually being at home even slimmer than usual—which was saying a lot. At this point, he hardly had any idea where she could be. That was it, actually, in a nutshell—with Gaia, there was no telling where she was at any point in time. He could only hope she hadn't left the state for some sort of secret search-and-rescue mission that he was as yet unaware of.

More than that, though, was how incredibly irritating Gaia's housemother, Suko, was. So officious. Icy, even. And she seemed to think he was some kind of borderline stalker, which made every encounter just that much more enjoyable.

The door swung open. *Bingo.* Suko stood, looking poised and unsurprised to see him. As usual. "May I help you?" she asked calmly, looking for all the world like that was the very last thing she wanted to do. Her thin lips were stretched over her teeth in an unconvincing facsimile of a smile.

I get it, I get it, Jake thought. *I've worn out my*

welcome. Point taken. But what do you want me to do?

Jake stuffed his hands into his pockets. "Is Gaia home?" he asked in as friendly and open a tone as he could muster.

Suko managed a quick head shake "no." "Gaia is out," she said, her tone disapproving. Technically, Suko didn't have jurisdiction over the comings and goings of her wards during the day as long as they respected their nightly curfew—and it seemed that there were ways to get around even that. But Suko made it clear that she thought Gaia was one accidental encounter away from being branded a common criminal. "You should call her if you need to speak with her," Suko offered, stepping backward and beginning to drag the door forward again, effectively shutting it in Jake's face.

"Hey—," Jake protested, stepping forward. Suko frowned. She obviously didn't like the idea of Jake forcing his way halfway into the house. Go figure.

"You should call her," Suko repeated, allowing irritation to creep into her tone. "She is not home."

"Wait!"

The door stopped about a fraction of an inch before its trajectory had finished. A gleaming, sooty eye pressed against the door, regarding Jake with scrutiny.

"I need to talk to him."

His Own Share of Shadowing

ZAN SHIMMIED OUT THROUGH THE tiny sliver of open door that Suko had—quite begrudgingly—left open. She smiled tentatively at Jake and pulled the door fully shut behind her. "Can we talk?" she asked.

Jake shrugged and copped a squat on the front steps. "Why the hell not?" he said resignedly. "Not like Gaia's going to be around anytime in the near future, is she?" He ran his fingers through his hair, feeling tired, frustrated, and above all worried about his girlfriend.

"I have no idea what Gaia's schedule is," Zan said. "I'd tell you if I did, honestly, but I can't."

Jake turned to regard Zan, finally, with measured curiosity. She seemed oddly subdued. He had met Zan a bunch of times by now, since she was always home when he came around. Near as he could tell, just about all she did was sit around the boardinghouse riding one high or another. Maybe late at night she went trawling for underground parties or something, but that was just speculation.

But he'd never seen her like this. He'd seen Zan high or hungover, fed up or flirtatious, daring or dismissive. Above all, Zan always seemed pretty attracted to Jake. Now she was acting like she was sitting next to her brother's friend or something. Her baby brother's friend... someone she was *worried* about.

"Um, so, what's up?" Jake began nervously.

Zan's gaze darted up and down Bank Street—anywhere but back at Jake. "So, I wanted to tell you that I, uh... I saw you today."

"You *saw* me? Where? Were you *following* me?" True, Jake had been doing his own share of shadowing lately, but he hadn't expected this news from Zan, of all people.

"No—no way, man," Zan said. "You think I don't have better things to do?" she asked, flipping her hair defiantly, suddenly seeming more like herself. "Please. No, I mean, I was in the park today, you know, scoring. From God. And I saw you."

Jake flinched. Here he'd thought he was being so subtle that Oliver would be so proud, and meanwhile he'd been discovered by a total burnout? How embarrassing. "Okay, yeah, so?" he asked gruffly, feeling a little humiliated.

"Well, no, that's not really the point," she amended quickly. "I mean, I did see you. But the thing is—so did God."

Now Jake was concerned. "Huh?" he asked in disbelief.

"Yeah," Zan continued somberly. "I know you were trying to be incognito or whatever"—and that, more than anything, really stung—"but I saw you, and I saw God see you, too."

"Well, did God *say* or *do* anything to indicate to you that he had seen me?" Jake asked, growing more defensive by the minute.

"Well, no. I didn't want him to *know* that I had seen you, so I was sort of trying to pretend that I hadn't," Zan explained, her voice shaking.

"So then you can't be sure," Jake finished, his face stony. His embarrassment had taken over, the voice of reason temporarily tamped down by his monstrous pride.

"Jake," Zan said slowly, "I'm sure."

She laid a hand on his knee. It was an utterly platonic gesture, so unlike her typical overt behavior that Jake felt even more unsettled. He shook her off.

"Well, thanks for the warning, Zan, but you know—I mean, half the time you don't even know what *day* it is, so I guess I can't be bothered to worry too much about what you *think* you saw," he snapped.

"Jake, it's true, I don't always have it all together—"

Jake snorted.

"But there's one thing I do know," she continued, ignoring his increasingly boorish behavior, "and for better or for worse, it's dealers. Now, I don't know if I would ever have told you that you need to look out for God. But in this case, you've seen him. I know you recognized him. And he recognized you, too. And that could be bad, Jake. Like, lose-a-finger bad. You need to listen to me."

Jake was done listening. He stood up abruptly, brushing dust off his jeans. "No, Zan, what I *need* is to find Gaia, to talk to her about *real* problems, real issues that she and I are dealing with. What I need to do is not to waste the rest of the day listening to you babble about things that you don't know the first thing about."

"But I do, Jake—I know about—," Zan started, desperate.

But Jake was already down the stairs and on his way.

Here's the thing—just now? When I told Zan I wasn't worried? That I could handle things?

Yeah, I lied.

First off, there's the fact that however unimpressive Chris Rodke is in the hallways at school, as God this guy's got serious power. I mean, he's got half the city—at least—literally eating out of his hand. Then there's the fact that Oliver seems to think he could be a threat. No idle words, that warning. And finally, there's Zan. The fact that the girl dragged herself together enough to sustain a coher-ent train of thought on my behalf. . . well, that does say something. And it sure does freak me out.

I don't know what exactly to "do" about this. I know Oliver and his team are on it, and thank God for that. All I can do is keep aware, be on the lookout, be on the defensive. Be prepared for anything. Because now, well. . . I think I just may have found the trouble that I was looking for.

SKYLER PUSHED OPEN THE DOOR TO

45 Bleecker at Bowery—room 312. As expected, his father was there—but all alone.

Right-Hand Man

"Dad, I thought this was a meeting?" Skyler asked, puzzled.

Dr. Rodke put down the file that he'd been scrutinizing and gestured for Skyler to come farther into the room. "Please, come in and sit down. We'll be meeting with the rest of the team as expected in room 314 but just a little later. I wanted you to come early. I wanted us to have a chance to talk."

Skyler eyed his father warily and slid into the seat directly to his father's right. God, did he love it—he was literally his father's right-hand man. There was actually a right-hand seat for the right-hand man. It was beautiful. He was glad, too, that his father had called him in. After all, ever since his phone conversation with Chris, well. . . he had some things of his own to discuss. "What's up?" he asked plaintively.

"It's Chris," Dr. Rodke said, his voice laced with thick anger.

Skyler straightened in his seat, instantly alert. "Tell me," he said.

"Nothing serious, son, nothing we have to be

excessively concerned about, but it's no secret that your brother's jealousy is growing every day."

"It's so ridiculous," Skyler scoffed.

"True, yes, he is being utterly ridiculous. But we can't completely dismiss him out of hand. The point is, he's becoming a bit of a squeaky wheel, and I'm afraid that before long, he'll be going after the oil."

Skyler drummed his fingers against the polished wood conference table. "You think he's a threat to us."

Dr. Rodke laughed as though the notion were completely insane. "Not quite. He has a long way to go before he's a threat," he said. "But we should keep an eye on him. A sharp watch. As I said, his discontent is palpable, and I wouldn't want to underestimate his capabilities. After all we've done and how hard we've worked, I wouldn't want his immature games to be our own undoing. Nothing can interfere with this deal—with the release of Invince. He's done a great job of getting the drug out onto the street at base level, but he's getting antsy. And I'm charging you with keeping him in line."

Memo

From: L
To: Field staff
Re: Invince

The following information has been confirmed:

First, that Rodke and Simon Pharmaceuticals is in fact looking to create a drug that suppresses the fear gene among humans.

Second, that a beta model of the drug has been leaked to the street, most likely to test its efficacy among unwitting human subjects.

Third, that subject Genesis is much sought after on the basis of her unique genetic makeup.

The questions at hand are:

1. For what purpose is the drug being developed? Surely the Rodkes have a buyer in mind. We must know everything.

2. In what ways will the final chemical differ from the beta model? What, in fact, are the beta model's side effects?

3. Do they have G's DNA? Are they anywhere near getting it?

The pieces of the puzzle are coming together, gentlemen, and once the above questions have been answered, the end will be in sight. What we are still lacking, however, is proof. Concrete proof. Lab reports, test results, tissue samples, chemical samples. A pill. Has someone actually thought to get their hands on a tab of beta Invince? Has someone tried it?

Come now, gentlemen. We're in the home stretch.

314. GAIA LOOKED AT THE DOORKNOB
of the room. This was it,
no doubt about it.

Small-Scale Endeavor

The door was slightly ajar. This all couldn't have been any stranger. For starters, this wasn't Rodke headquarters, but it wasn't some skanky downtown warehouse, either. It was an actual medical facility. She had no idea what type of dealings went on here—at the front desk she'd encountered a bored-looking security guard flipping idly through a magazine. She'd quickened her stride as she walked past him and tried to look confident. As though there was no question that she belonged here. As she had maneuvered down the hallways, she had seen one nurse hurrying along carrying a tray of test tubes.

But that was it. No high-tech surveillance, no state-of-the-art technology. This place looked like a legit medical office, albeit a small-scale endeavor. Where the hell was she?

She touched her toe against the door lightly, testing it. It swung open. Gaia held her breath and flattened herself against the wall of the hallway, prepared at any moment for a gaggle of men in white lab coats to come swarming out of the room, screaming for her blood.

It didn't happen.

She slowly, ever so slowly inched her body into the room, taking it in. There was nothing of note about it. It looked like a conference room. In the center of the room stood a huge, polished wooden table surrounded by chairs. A dismal-looking potted plant lay wilting in the corner. *Places to hide,* Gaia thought, looking around. *I don't have much time.*

There!

At the far side of the room, behind the table, stood a row of cabinets. The cabinets were at least four feet tall. Granted, Gaia was taller than that, but she could squeeze. She was flexible. She quickly crossed over to the cabinets and opened one of the doors.

Just as she suspected, the shelves inside were empty and spaced several feet apart. Jackpot.

Thank God I'm not claustrophobic, Gaia thought, lowering herself onto her belly and sliding onto the first shelf. Okay, she didn't necessarily *need* to chill out there all night, so it would do. She pulled the doors toward her with enough force that they slammed shut once she'd yanked her fingers out of the way. Though a broken nail would have been a small, worthwhile price to pay.

For a few excruciating moments all Gaia heard in the darkness was the sound of her own ragged breath. She willed herself calm. So far she had seen only two people in this place—neither of whom seemed especially dangerous. No reason to assume that would change. After all, hadn't she basically just sauntered in off the street?

Yeah, good logic, she told herself. It was BS, she knew. She had no idea what to expect from Skyler's little meeting. She had to be prepared for anything.

Gaia heard the sound of the door swinging open and stiffened. *Here we go,* she thought. She heard footsteps—three, no, four men striding heavily into the room. Four chairs scraped against the floor as they were pulled out from under the table. Four grown men lowering themselves into their seats.

"Gentlemen, we're here to make a deal." Gaia's ears pricked up. It was Dr. Rodke.

"As you know, the test compounds of I-23C have been reported fully successful by our lab technicians. The drug is ready to be tested on human subjects."

Gaia recognized the speaker as Dr. Ulrich, the man who had performed her genetic modification. What drug? There was a drug? Had her surgery been part of a larger scheme? She remembered Oliver's warnings to her just before she'd gone under and felt ashamed. True, she'd had good reason to doubt his sincerity. But she'd never forgive herself if she had allowed her own curiosity to be the cause of dangerous developments in gene splicing—or whatever else Rodke and Ulrich were up to.

"Our success in creating fear was instrumental in our success in suppressing it," Ulrich continued, sending shivers down Gaia's spine. *Their success in creating fear. . .* , she mused. *Me. They're talking about me.*

I'm a part of this.

That's *why Skyler's been keeping me so close. He must need something more from me.*

The thought made Gaia shudder with anger. It was all she could do not to burst out from the cabinet and pummel Ulrich. She tightened her hands into fists and clenched her jaw.

"And what about this beta model—this Invince that's been on the streets?" This was someone Gaia couldn't place.

"Invince is an early version of our lab compound that was leaked onto the streets for more reliable results among human subjects. It was a deliberate effort by our team," Dr. Rodke said smoothly.

Gaia fumed. Dr. Rodke was responsible for Invince? That meant he was responsible for the recent wave of daredevil crimes and violence that had swept the city. That meant he was responsible for the skinheads who had come after Gaia. And the thugs who attacked *Ed*! But why? At what cost? What was it all for?

Gaia didn't have to wait long to get her answer. And when she did, it made her blood run cold.

"I-23C is ready for the soldiers, sir," Skyler said, his voice ringing with pride. "With Invince in their bloodstreams, your army will be unstoppable."

Free will. It's an interesting concept. Human beings choose to believe that they have some level of agency over the course of their lives, some measure of control. But that's all it is—a measure. An ineffectual effort to assert power over circumstances far beyond any of our reach. And it's true of us all, no matter where we stand on the social spectrum. While a child trapped, without resource or advantage, in the inner city is likely to know a lifetime of dis- enfranchisement, the grandest dame of the Junior League is equally a product of social expectations, of the conventions of her peers, of the culture of consumerism. It's a paradox—those with the most capi- tal are often those least free, burdened as they are by a need to acquire, to compete. . . to spend. This fierce drive toward commer- cialism shifts the power dynamic away from them.

Shifting the power, of course, directly toward me.

I may be young, I may be reasonably inexperienced, but I've
learned a few things of late. For
starters, people are pawns. A
blunt, harsh fact but true nonetheless. Just pawns, waiting mind-
lessly to be pointed toward the
next big Thing. Create a product,
create a demand for the product,
and you've manipulated a wave of
shameless, unthinking automatons.
Automatons on a quest for some
Thing. Some Thing like Invince.

Of course, New Yorkers hardly
need another drug. After all, most
of the people in my life have
unlimited access to Valium, Xanax,
Prozac, Paxil. . . . High school
kids pop these like candy; pre-
scriptions aren't even necessary
anymore. Or if you can't get a pre-
scription, you can always nick a
few doses from your mother's hand-
bag without her noticing, right?
Nowadays everyone's been diagnosed
with attention deficit disorder.
Heck, back during my days at sleep-
away camp, I felt left out at
lunchtime, being the only camper

not shuttled off to the nurse to take my meds. The Village School idiots take Ritalin recreationally! And these are only the legal drugs. It's true: we *are* a Prozac nation. And we're constantly on the lookout for the next fix.

And if our choices in drug abuse are any indication, we're a pretty freaking insecure bunch. Antidepressants, antianxietals. . . Everyone just wants to make bad feelings go away. And *everyone*, just about everyone in New York City, is prepared to pay top dollar to feel, well. . . fearless.

I can help.

My father, the amazing Dr. Rodke, would have you believe that *he's* the go-to guy. That he knows how to make the monsters hiding under the bed—*poof*—disappear. And yes, he's a science man, a man with the answers. Some of the things he's been able to do in his lab, some of his discoveries regarding genetic manipulation, have been profound. He, of course, is looking to create the ultimate

antianxietal. And he's coming
close with Invince. Invince has
the power to completely suppress
fear, and he's going to bring it
to the masses.

That's where I come in.

You may think that I'm bitter
or jealous, a victim of extreme
sibling rivalry. It's okay—you
can think that. You'd be right.

I'm not sure quite where or when
it began, this intense need to
outdo my brother. When I came out,
I never worried that my sexual
identity might drive a wedge
between myself and my father; I
never minded Skyler taking on the
role of alpha male. No, this need
to outdo my brother, to succeed by
triumphing *over* him—that compulsion
was firmly in place well before I
knew what being "out" meant.

My father tells me not to
worry; he tells me there's enough
of the Rodke fortune to go
around, and sure, I reap the benefits in the form of a chauf-
feured car anytime I want or the
ability to purchase whatever,

whenever. But it's not enough.

I know my father is grooming Skyler to be the heir apparent. But the way I see it, that job belongs to me. And I'm not going to settle for less; I'm not interested in being the also-ran. Money is nice, but as I've stated before, it isn't power. My father is getting ready to hand over the power, or at the very least to share it—and not with me. And I am not going to stand for it. But I'm not sure what to do to turn things around.

They're looking to edge me out. It's obvious. I don't know why they think their late-night chats in my father's office are so subtle. I don't know why my father doesn't realize how much investigating I do down at his labs. Maybe it's a good thing, then, in this case at least, that my father pays me so little attention. Because they don't know about me.

They know I'm God, sure. But what they *don't* know is that God's got plans of his own. While I'm out peddling their second-rate,

beta-model drug to the masses—
raising demand—I'm brainstorming.
Troubleshooting. I'm making plans.

Because I've got the goods.
And I'm going to take them down.

And if anyone—and I do mean anyone—had any plans to undermine me—
well, now, that just won't do. And
I'm talking to you, Jake Montone.

I know you saw me. I know you
think I *didn't* see you. You won't
let yourself believe that I could
be as smooth as you. That's your
tragic flaw, my friend—your hubris.
That's going to be your undoing.

Because I'll be damned if I'll
let you get between me and my self-
determined fate. I'm no common
street dealer, true—but in many ways
I'm worse. In many ways I have much
more at stake. Trust me on this,
Jake, and don't give me any trouble.
I have no problems going after you.

If anything—or anyone—is going
to compromise my identity, well,
wait and see, my friend. . . .

I'll just have to exact a little divine intervention.

Enough is enough.

Will people never learn? I don't know how to get the point across. My missing fear gene? Yeah, it comes in handy. I like to be all brave and straightforward, but it's not a fabulous treat, and it's *not* something I would wish on someone else. Not even my own worst enemy. And believe me, I've got a lot of enemies.

People have already tried to harness my "power." Specifically, Loki tried. And all he got for it was a big, honking coma. My friend Heather wanted to be fearless. Now she's blind. It's time to face reality, people: human beings were intended to experience fear.

Sure, it's easy enough to understand why someone might want to create an army of fearless warriors. But I think, in some cases, fear actually propels people, motivates them, drives them to work harder.

Of course, I digress. My point really is that any attempt to

suppress fear scientifically has
up until now failed. Big time.
And I think it's safe to say that
Loki had a team of experts on his
side while he worked. So it's
hard to see why Dr. Rodke thinks
he'll be more successful. The
gene manipulation he put me
through wore off. He doesn't get
it. He doesn't get that I am a
freak of nature, not to be dupli-
cated in science.

He doesn't get that no matter
how close he gets, I'm going to
stop him.

I'm going to stop him, and then,
quite possibly, I'm going to pummel
him. Because frankly, as I said
before, enough is enough. I'm really,
really tired. Tired of all my loved
ones coming to tragic ends. Tired of
not being able to trust anyone's
motives. Tired of constantly being in
danger. So I'm going to take Rodke and
Simon Pharmaceuticals down. I don't
know how, exactly, but believe you me,
it's going to happen. Dr. Rodke, . . .
Skyler. Chris and Liz, if they're in
on it. I hope to God she's not; I'd

like to think that I have known at
least one or two true friends in my
lifetime, but if she is, so help me,
I'll take her down, too.

And once that's done, I'm out
of here. A fresh start, a clean
slate, greener pastures—pick your
metaphor. I've hit my breaking
point. I've had enough.

It's over.

**Read an excerpt from the second book
in the hot new series**

the nine lives of chloe king

VOLUME TWO

The Stolen

by
CELIA THOMSON

Two

"What do we do *now*?"

Paul bent over; there was a stitch in his side and he was puffing like an asthmatic. He only smoked once or twice a week—this was probably just plain old-fashioned out-of-shape-ness. He put his hand on his belly and straightened up. Amy was standing stiff as a rod, breathing normally, hands on her hips, glaring at him like the whole thing was his fault.

Behind them another helicopter was circling the bridge. They had been hovering like pissed-off dragonflies off and on since Friday night. Paul and Amy hoped that the National Guard had caught up to Chloe and whoever was attacking her and split them up—but almost a day had passed, and it didn't look like there had been any resolution.

Paul thought he'd seen a body fall from the bridge, but he didn't say anything about it to Amy.

"Well?" his girlfriend demanded again.

Paul sighed.

"I don't know—what do *you* think we should do?"

"Call her mom . . . ?" But even as she suggested it, Amy trailed off, knowing that it probably wasn't the right thing to do—or, more importantly, that it wasn't what Chloe would want. She ran her hands through her chestnut hair in exasperation, pulling on the roots. It was a leftover habit from when she was younger and tried to flatten her big, often frizzy hair every chance she got. "What do you think it was all about—*really*?"

They'd had this conversation several times in the last twenty-four hours, but somehow Amy was never satisfied with Paul's answers.

"I don't know. Drugs? Gangs? Some weird psycho game of tag?"

"Maybe it's got to do with her real parents or something. Maybe she's actually some sort of Russian Mafia princess."

Paul gave her a lopsided smile. Silently they started to walk home, not holding hands or anything. Like they had in the old days, when the three of them were just good friends. Before Chloe almost died from falling off Coit Tower. Before she and Amy got into that weird little snit they were in for days—and had just patched up. Before Chloe started seeing Alyec and Brian . . .

"You know," Paul said slowly, "a *lot* of weird shit has happened with Chloe in the last couple of months, don't you think?"

Amy shrugged. "Seems to me she got her period and turned into a total bitch. For a while, at least," she added hastily. Chloe might have been a bitch, but she was still Amy's best friend, and she was still missing.

"No, it's more than that." Paul frowned, crinkling his long white forehead. "I mean like her fall and the bruises on her face and her random absences from school—not to mention being totally incommunicado about general Chloe life issues."

"She was going to tell us everything," Amy remembered. "On the bridge . . . She was just about to explain *something*. . . ."

". . .when that freak with knives showed up." They looked at each other for a long moment.

"We were talking about her crush on *Alyec* when she jumped off Coit Tower," Amy suddenly pointed out.

"She didn't jump, she fell," Paul said, surprised at the way Amy said that. She was the only person on the planet who probably knew Chloe better than he did, and it was a really weird thing to say about their friend. At no point in her life, even at her gothiest moments, had Chloe *ever* seemed the suicidal sort. *A jackass, sometimes, but never suicidal.* Jumping up onto the ledge to get more attention had been a *little* rash, but they had been drinking, and it wasn't completely out of the range of typical Chloe behavior.

"Whatever," Amy said quickly, dismissing it. "Her life started going crazy after that. I'll bet it has something to do with him."

"That's insane. How could *thinking* about him have anything to do with getting mugged or whatever?" Paul asked. He tried not to laugh or smile but couldn't stop his dark eyes from twinkling. Fortunately Amy wasn't looking directly at him.

"No! Think about it." She began ticking off facts on the tips of her black glitter fingernails. "She was mugged right after we all split up at The Raven, then became a total hag when she started actually dating Alyec—and he's Russian, just like her. Maybe he's got her into something *bad.*"

"What about *Brian*, then?" Paul demanded. "As long as we're accusing random people of having somehow screwed up Chloe's life and sent assassins after her. Brian, the mysterious sort-of boyfriend who never kissed her, who isn't in school, and, most importantly— *who we've never seen?*"

Amy stared at him with blank blue eyes, at a loss for an answer. He was about to add a few more salient facts that proved she was a complete wacko with insubstantial—*crazy*—arguments, but then he noticed Amy's lips trembling and tears forming on her lower lids.

"She'll be okay. The National Guard is out there. We can call the police if you want or her mom later—let's say if we haven't heard from her in a few hours. Okay?"

Amy nodded miserably, and they continued walking home.

Three

Amy looked into the bottom of her locker hopefully. Nope, nothing. She was always making cute little notes for Paul and slipping them into *his* locker. Sometimes they were quick scrawls—*See you in English!*—and sometimes they were really intricate things she made the night before with cloth and her glue gun and stuff.

Not. Once. Had he ever done the same for her. She didn't want to outright *ask*—but how strongly did a girl have to hint? Now that she was finally dating a nice, nonpsycho boy, she figured she should cash in on some of the perks that were supposed to go along with it. She was being stupid, she knew, and selfish: Paul did all other kinds of nice boyfriendy things, like buying tickets ahead of time for movies they wanted to see and getting her a coffee at the café if she asked. And he would talk to her for *hours* on the phone about all sorts of things. . . .

But once, just once, Amy wished someone would treat her exactly the way she wanted them to. All that jazz about the Golden Rule and karma and stuff—her do-gooding didn't exactly seem like it was making its way back to her yet.

She closed the door dejectedly. Then she kicked it, hard enough to leave a dent with her steel-toed combat boots. Things were so up in the air and uncertain these days. Chloe was still gone. Amy cursed herself for not hearing the phone when she'd called; it had been jammed at the bottom of her backpack and she had been outside, looking for Chloe, of all people. Amy started checking her voice mail about a thousand times an hour, hoping to hear something from her friend, but nothing.

She was definitely worried about Chloe. No doubt about it.

But she also felt a little . . . left behind. It was like she had made the decision to go out with Paul and now all these strange and mysterious things were going on in Chloe's life that Amy *still* wasn't in on. . . .

Alyec's famous barking laugh echoed down the hall. Amy looked: he was slamming his locker closed and waving goodbye to his friends Keira and Halley—very non-Chloe friends—and balancing his flute case on top of his notebook. *Off for a music lesson.*

Amy realized this was her perfect opportunity to thoroughly interrogate the untrustworthy jerk. She snuck along twenty feet behind him, keeping her back to the lockers, Harriet the Spy style. She needn't have bothered, though: Alyec was too busy waving to people in the main corridor to notice her.

As soon as he turned down toward the music wing, Amy double-timed her tiptoeing until she was almost four feet behind him. She didn't have to do it *too* quickly, though: he was dragging one of his legs a little. *What is that, some kind of new cool-guy walk?*

She smoothed her big dark red hair back and put on her best frowny face. She wished she could do the cold-blue-eyed thing—she had the eyes for it, after all—but somewhere between her freckles and "aristocratic" nose, she tended to come across more goofy and pleasant than aloof.

"You could just, I don't know, talk to me like a normal person," Alyec said causally, without looking behind him.

After she got over her surprise, Amy was so angry at being caught out she almost stamped her foot.

"*Where's Chloe?!*" she demanded. "I swear to *God*, Alyec Ilychovich, if you fucking *hurt* her . . . !"

A couple of students toting big, cumbersome instrument cases turned the corner, giggling and holding sheet music.

Alyec easily scooped an arm around Amy and pulled her into an empty practice room. He put his hand over her mouth and held a finger to his own. He stood there, his ice blue eyes locked on her own blue ones, insisting that she stay quiet until the two other students had passed.

He watched out the door to see if anyone else was coming and then took his hand away from her mouth.

"If you're not going to talk to me normally," Alyec said with a faint smile, "at least don't go throwing a psycho fit about it in public."

The room was mostly dark, on an inside wing with no windows. It was small and cluttered with the sort of desks and chairs small groups of students would sit in while practicing. In just a few minutes some teacher would come in and flip on the lights and the next period would begin. But for now it was just the two of them, and they were very alone. Alyec's chiseled-perfect face was inches from Amy's.

"You . . . *jerk*!" Amy lifted up her foot to stamp on his toes. He very neatly spun her away so she was at arm's length.

"She is home sick today, that is all," he said patiently.

That was what all the teachers had said when Amy had asked them, too.

"I *know* she said she was safe, but I *saw* what happened on the bridge," Amy said, sticking out her chin.

Alyec's blue eyes widened, and for once he didn't have a comeback.

"What's all this about?" she demanded. "Why was someone trying to kill Chloe? Twice? You know. I *know* you know."

He opened his mouth, looking for something to say. "She really is just sick at home. With her mother," he repeated lamely.

There was a long, tense moment between them, Amy glaring at him, *daring* him to lie again. He finally looked away.

Amy slammed her fist up into his stomach.

"*Jerk!*" she said again, stamping out into the hallway as he leaned over, hand to his belly. She knew she couldn't have done any real damage with her small wrists and the "artist's hands" that Chloe always made fun of, but at least he looked surprised. Amy spun around.

"Chloe is my best. Friend. *Ever*," she hissed. "If anything happens to her because of you, I'm getting my cousin Steve to beat the living *shit* out of you—and anyone else you know!"

She turned and left, adrenaline—if not exactly triumph—ringing in her ears.

Four

Chloe was snoozing, *The History of the Mai* resting on her lap, its old leather cover making her sneeze occasionally in her sleep. This was her second time trying to get through the dense text since she'd arrived, and the second time it had put her promptly to sleep.

She was dreaming again. This time a cat as large as a person walked toward her quietly. Chloe waited for it to tell her something useful or do something. . . .

"Am I disturbing you?" it said.

Chloe jumped, finally awake. She was *not* dreaming. The weird and ghostly visage that had terrified her the night before was standing patiently before her. *That's just Kim; she's a freak,* Alyec had said.

And boy, was he right.

She was a skinny and oddly built girl, willowy and sleek. Her hair was shorter than Chloe's, shiny, full, and black—almost blue-black, almost Asian. She had high cheekbones.

And velvety black cat ears.

Big ones. The size they would be if a cat's head were blown up to human proportions.

Her eyes were an unreal green, slit like a cat's, completely alien and lacking the appearance of normal human emotion. She wore a normal black tunic-length sweater and black jeans. She was barefoot; her bony toes had claws at the end and little tufts of black fur. Chloe couldn't help thinking about hobbits, except the girl was drop-dead gorgeous. She seemed about Chloe's age, but it was hard to tell.

"Uh, no, I was supposed to be reading anyway," Chloe said, running a hand over her face, trying not to stare.

"I'm afraid I gave you a bit of a scare when you arrived. I'm sorry—I do not usually expect, new, ah, people to be wandering around late at night."

"Hey, uh, no problem. My bad." Chloe kept on trying to look elsewhere, not sure what to say, still trying not to stare.

"I am—"

"Kim, yeah, Alyec told me."

The other girl looked annoyed. "My name is *Kemet* or Kem, *not* Kim. No one calls me that, though, thanks to people like Alyec." She sighed, sinking gracefully into the chair next to Chloe. "*Kemet* means 'Egypt.' Where we are from originally, thousands of years ago."

Chloe made a note to ask her about that later, but something else intrigued her more.

"Is that your given name?"

"No." Kim stared at the floor. "My given name is Greska."

"Oh." Chloe tried not to smile.

"You can see why I wanted to change it."

"Absolutely."

There was a moment of silence. Kim was looking into Chloe's face as curiously as Chloe was trying to avoid staring at the other girl.

"So we're from Egypt originally?" Chloe asked, trying to break Kim's icy, blinkless gaze. She closed the book. "I . . . uh . . . hadn't even gotten that far."

"We're first recorded, or history first mentions us there: 'Beloved of Bastet and guarded by Sekhmet.'" Kim took the book up and flipped to a page with a map on it and an inscription in hieroglyphs. "We were created by her, according to legend."

Chloe didn't know where to begin with her questions—*Created by? Kim is my age and she can read ancient Egyptian writing?*

"Most of us in this pride are from Eastern Europe—"

"Wait, 'pride'?"

"Yes." The girl looked up at her coolly. If she'd had a tail, it would have been thumping impatiently. "That is the congregation our people travel in. Like lions."

"And Sergei is the leader of the . . . Pride?"

"No, just this one in California. There are four in the New World. Well, were. The one in the East is also primarily made up of Eastern European Mai." Kim flipped a few pages and showed another map with statistics and inscriptions, lines and arrows originating from Africa and pointing toward different places: migration routes to lower Africa, Europe, and farther east. "The pride in New Orleans tends to be made up of Mai who stayed in sub-Saharan Africa the longest. They like the heat," she added with a disapproving twitch of her nose.

"And the fourth one?"

"It was . . . lost," Kim said diffidently. "Anyway, we have been driven all over the world, away from our homes. Our pride managed to live in Abkhazia for several hundred years after we left the Middle East for good." She pointed to a little area shaded pink to the northwest of Russia, on the Black Sea. "The people there remained polytheistic long after the Roman Empire declined, Christianity swept the world, and Baghdad was destroyed by the Mongols."

"I get the feeling that there's a 'but' in here somewhere. . . ."

"Many Abkhazians were driven out in the middle of the nineteenth century to Turkey by domestic warfare with the Georgians. We got caught up in it and families separated, some staying, some fleeing, some going to the Ukraine or St. Petersburg. And then again, not so long ago, just when some started to move back and reunite with lost branches, there was new violence."

She put the book down and twitched her nose

again—more like a rabbit than a cat, Chloe decided. It seemed to signal a change in emotion.

"I'm an orphan, just like you," the girl continued bluntly. "My parents were killed or separated during the Georgian-inspired violence in 1988, before the Wall fell. They say I had . . . a sister . . . ," she said slowly, looking at Chloe with hope. "A year older than me. When I saw you come in, I thought we looked alike— and . . . maybe . . ."

Maybe a little, except for the ears, was Chloe's first, defensive reaction. If you took away the ears, they actually *did* look a little similar: dark hair, fair skin, light eyes, high cheekbones.

What if it were true? Chloe had *always* wanted a sibling, especially a sister; Amy was the closest she had, but it still wasn't quite the same, like someone you could whisper to in the middle of the night or talk about your crazy parents with. Someone who you could scream at when she borrowed your favorite piece of clothing without telling you and then brought it back reeking of cigarette smoke or just plain ruined.

Someone who could tell you it was okay when you suddenly grew claws.

So maybe she's a little freaky, but a sister is a sister. . . .

As many as 1 in 3 Americans
who have HIV...don't know it.

TAKE CONTROL.
KNOW YOUR STATUS.
GET TESTED.

To learn more about HIV testing,
or get a free guide to HIV and
other sexually transmitted diseases:

www.knowhivaids.org
1-866-344-KNOW

FEARLESS™

THE END OF AN ERA IS NEAR. . . .
BE AFRAID.

You've watched Gaia break legs.

You've watched her get her heart broken.

But you've never seen her
break free quite like this.

Gaia's high school days are numbered.
And once they've run out, Gaia will
make her most dangerous choice yet.

DON'T MISS THE FINAL ADVENTURE
IN THE BEST-SELLING SERIES:

Available November 2004

And coming soon:
FEARLESS FBI

Published by Simon Pulse